I Know
Who Likes You

DOUG COONEY

Aladdin Paperbacks

New York   London   Toronto   Sydney

Also by Doug Cooney
The Beloved Dearly

ALADDIN PAPERBACKS
An imprint of Simon & Schuster Children's Publishing Division
1230 Avenue of the Americas, New York, NY 10020
Copyright © 2004 by Doug Cooney
All rights reserved, including the right of reproduction in whole or in part in any form.
ALADDIN PAPERBACKS and colophon are registered trademarks of Simon & Schuster, Inc.
Also available in a Simon & Schuster Books for Young Readers hardcover edition.
Designed by Lucy Ruth Cummins
The text of this book was set in Joanna MT.
Manufactured in the United States of America
First Aladdin Paperbacks edition August 2005
2 4 6 8 10 9 7 5 3 1
The Library of Congress has cataloged the hardcover edition as follows:
Cooney, Doug.
I know who likes you / Doug Cooney.
p. cm.
Summary: When Swimming Pool's mother insists she graduate from charm school or give up baseball, Ernie, who is the reluctant team manager, and Dusty, the catcher, pull together to help the team and their friend.
ISBN 0-689-85419-6 (hc.)
[1. Baseball—Fiction. 2. Etiquette—Fiction. 3. Friendship—Fiction. 4. Schools—Fiction.] I. Title.
PZ7.C78371k 2004
[Fic]—dc21 2003004531
ISBN 1-4169-0261-9 (pbk.)

For CCML

The author gratefully acknowledges Derek Anderson, Ellia Bisker, Charlotte Booker, Carling Boyles, David Gale, Christian Lebano, Shawn Levy, Melanie Ryan, and the many creative artists of all ages who have contributed their energy and spirit to this story.

CONTENTS

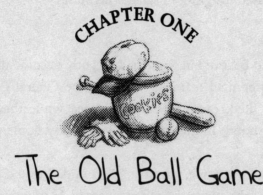

CHAPTER ONE

The Old Ball Game

Ernie had been totally bamboozled.

In his wildest dreams, Ernie never saw himself standing under the sweltering sun in the far right outfield of the old ballpark during the bottom of the eighth inning in a stand-off between the Central Comets and the Bayside Bulldogs. Ernie was absolutely miserable.

"I don't even like baseball!" Ernie hollered to no one in particular. "I got no business in baseball!"

Normally kids in the outfield are happy to make the most of their isolated post by peppering the air with lame jokes like "Betty Crocker makes a better batter!" Some kids bleat "Naaaaah!" like sheep in a pasture. Other kids wag their hips to a chant of "hey-batter, batter-batter-batter, swwiiiing!"

Ernie didn't do any of that. Ernie just yelled whatever was on his mind and stomped in the grass to the beat of his own sulk. "Baseball is boring," he wailed. "Boring, boring—OW!" A salty drop of sweat caught Ernie in the eye and he winced in pain. "Great!" Ernie bellowed, sending a growl across the outfield. "Now I'm sweating! And I now got an itch!" He used his glove to scratch his rump.

It is hard to believe but Ernie had recently become the new and self-appointed team manager for the Central Comets. His father, Red, came up with the idea while they were hogging a booth in a pizza joint on the way home from a movie.

"Come on, Ernie, admit it," Red said. "It's the perfect position to take advantage of your natural-born tendency to want to run the whole show!"

"Team manager?" asked Ernie, somewhat skeptical.

"Gotta a nice ring, don't it?" Red urged, reaching for another slice of pizza.

"Yeah, but," Ernie hedged, "I don't exactly like baseball very much. And I'm not very good at it either."

"Who cares!" said Red. He jabbed his pizza slice at Ernie to deliver the payoff punch. "You won't get near the baseball! You'll be team manager!"

"Team manager," Ernie repeated once more, imitating his father's enthusiasm. Ernie had to agree. It had a nice ring.

Not everyone was so enthusiastic about the idea. Kip, team

captain for the Comets, wasn't exactly thrilled when Ernie suddenly showed up at practice to announce, "I'm team manager because my father says I get to be team manager and if I can't be team manager, I'm going home."

"Team manager?" Kip groused at the time. "Never had a 'team manager.'" He glanced at the other Comets on the field and scratched his head. "What's a team manager anyway?" he asked.

No one seemed to know the answer to that question. Nothing in the league rulebook addressed the subject of team managers. In fact, none of the grown-ups that comprised the Comets' rotating roster of coaches, chauffeurs, chaperones, and umpires had any experience with team managers at all.

"Now wait a minute," said Mrs. Morgenstern, who happened to be team coach that week, "I do seem to recall something about team managers but I remember it said team managers also have to play on the field." She placed a hand on Ernie's back and pushed him onto the baseball diamond.

"Whoa, whoa, whoa," Ernie protested but Mrs. Morgenstern had already chucked him a glove from the equipment duffel. "Do you want to be team manager or not?" she queried, with a look that expected to be obeyed. Ernie was backed into a corner. Just like that, Ernie's baseball career had begun.

As Ernie walked onto the field, all the Comets groaned. "Hey," Mrs. Morgenstern barked, "don't give me that! Are we going to play ball or not?"

The Comets deferred to Kip, the team captain, for an answer to that question. Kip kicked at the dirt. "Let's play ball!" he yelled, but it wasn't a happy moment. For quite some time, Kip and several other Comets had suspected that Mrs. Morgenstern made up the rules as she went along but so far no one had mustered the nerve to confront her or complain.

Later that afternoon, when Kip and several key Comets reconvened in the dugout to rehash the blow-by-blow of Ernie's unexpected arrival on their team, they agreed on two points: (1) Mrs. Morgenstern knew nothing about baseball; and (2) Ernie knew even less.

It was true. Ernie was hopeless at the game. He couldn't throw and he couldn't catch. Nobody actually said that Ernie "threw like a girl"—the Comets knew better than to say that—but Ernie certainly didn't throw the ball like he wanted it to go anywhere. When it came time to catch, Ernie would raise his glove into the air to offer a target and let the balls go whizzing past. He didn't even make an effort.

"He can't throw! Can't catch! He doesn't know the first thing about baseball!" Kip cried in desperation. Nobody argued the point. It took very little discussion for Kip and the Comets to decide to place Ernie in Outer Mongolia. That was their nickname for the far right outfield.

"Outer Mongolia, perfect!" said Kip. "The ball never goes there!" The Comets nodded conspiratorially in agreement. A kid could grow old in the outfield and never see the ball. They didn't feel particularly good about sending any kid to Outer Mongolia but they comforted themselves that it was for the good of the team.

"It's settled then," said Kip. "Bye-bye Ernie! Hello Outer

Mongolia! We'll never hear from that kid again!"

Unfortunately, the Comets had overlooked one thing. Ernie was loud.

"What am I doing here?" Ernie bellowed from the outfield. His voice was getting a little hoarse because he'd been hollering the whole game. "I can't throw! I can't catch! I don't know the first thing about baseball!"

"That's what you're doing in Outer Mongolia!" cracked Ronjon, the kid at shortstop, and he said it loud enough for Ernie to hear. A lot of Comets snickered and laughed. Ronjon was always making wisecracks like that.

"Ugh!" Ernie barked indignantly from the distance. He tugged off his glove to wipe his forehead on his sleeve but ended up whacking himself with the glove. In the process, his baseball cap flew off his head and landed a few feet away. Ernie groaned in exasperation and began sputtering under his breath about his seemingly endless deficiencies as a ball player. "I don't even look like a ball player!"

That was true. Ernie's uniform was too big and his glove was too small. He had to cinch the pants at the waist and the sleeves hung halfway down his arms. It looked as if Ernie were wearing his pajamas. To make matters worse, there was the issue of Ernie's cleats.

Ernie couldn't run in cleats. Whenever he tried, his cleats stuck in the dirt and Ernie fell flat on his face in the grass. It was like throwing beanbags at sitting ducks during the school carnival—one moment there, next moment gone. The sight was pathetic of course, whenever Ernie tripped over his own feet and fell smack to the ground, but it had happened so often that it was also getting to be really hysterical. To the Comets, it was comic relief.

And sure enough, the trick with the cleats is precisely what happened when Ernie trotted to retrieve his baseball cap. Still grumbling under his breath, Ernie took three steps, stumbled over his own feet, and dropped like a ton of bricks.

"There he goes!" hooted Ronjon, pointing at the outfield. "Now you see him, now you don't!" The Comets all laughed.

It was bad enough being stuck in the sweltering sun with no place to go and nothing to do. Ernie had suffered enough. He pushed himself to his feet, snatched his cap from the grass and whacked it against his leg.

"I can't take it anymore!" he hollered. "I'm supposed to be treated with respect! I'm supposed to be team manager! I'm supposed to be in an office with air-conditioning or something! I'm not supposed to be stuck in the field, itching and sweating and losing my mind!"

Ernie paused to see if his tantrum was having any effect. To the contrary, no one was listening. Kip caught a pop fly to first base. Another batter struck out and headed for the dugout, and the outfield and infield came in, anticipating a bunt. The game was going on entirely without Ernie. No one was listening to Ernie at all.

Ernie grunted with dissatisfaction. "We'll see about that," he muttered. He lifted his glove like a megaphone, took a deep breath and began to bellow as loud as he could.

"Swimming Pool!" he cried over and over until it became a chant. "Swim-ming Pool, Swim-ming Pool!"

CHAPTER TWO

Something of a Star

Ernie wasn't shouting "Swimming Pool" because of the sweltering sun. He was plenty hot in the outfield but that wasn't the reason. Ernie was shouting "Swimming Pool" because that was the name of the Comets' pitcher.

Swimming Pool stood on the pitcher's mound, working her evil eye on the next batter at the plate. Swimming Pool was the only girl on the field, but she stood a full inch taller than most of the boys. She also knew more about the history of baseball. This year alone, she had already logged three reports with the same title, "Abner Doubleday: Father of American Baseball." She could fire off batting averages and statistics like nobody's business.

But all that brain power was nothing compared to Swimming Pool's sheer skill. She simply had the best arm on

7

the team. "No debate," said Kip, the team captain, "no discussion." As far as Kip was concerned, if Swimming Pool wanted to be pitcher, the job was hers. And in truth, Swimming Pool had already established herself as something of a star among the Comets' fans.

People were always shouting "Swimming Pool" from the bleachers and with good reason. Swimming Pool put on a good show. She was always striking out batters, catching kids stealing third, and scooping up a triple play.

And sometimes, it's true, people shouted "Swimming Pool" for no reason at all. They just shouted her name because it was so much fun to say. "Swim-ming Pool! Swim-ming Pool!" A chant would get started and sweep across the bleachers like a wave. Swimming Pool made people happy.

Of course, Ernie wasn't so very happy when he shouted "Swimming Pool" from the outfield. Ernie was still miserable in his outpost and the chance to shout Swimming Pool's name hadn't changed that situation one bit. "Swimming Pool!" he continued to crow, adding four or five syllables to the word pool for good measure. "Swimming Pooooooooool!"

Unfortunately, this was not the best moment to interfere with Swimming Pool's concentration on the game.

As it so happened, Swimming Pool was about to launch her "Cincinnati Special." It was a special pitch, a patented secret weapon, and a signature whammy that she kept in reserve. Technically, the pitch was a combination fastball with a surprise curve at the end. Others have thrown the same pitch. But Swimming Pool delivered her "Cincinnati Special" with a particular showmanship and pizzazz—and there was no arguing with its success. The elaborate wind-up to the "Cincinnati Special" involved an elbow, a knee-hitch, and a deep, long stride that looked pretty funny on the mound but was still serious business considering the number of batters who had been sent back to the dugout because of it. Swimming Pool's "Cincinnati Special" required split-second timing and tremendous concentration, and it always delivered.

Normally, Swimming Pool reserved the "Cincinnati Special" for those occasions—when the game was tight or the crowd was bored or the batter was especially annoying. But the catcher had signaled for the "Cincinnati Special" and Swimming Pool completely trusted the kid at home plate.

Swimming Pool had hand-picked Dusty to be her catcher. At first glance, Dusty seemed like an unlikely choice for that position. He was a curious half-pint kid with a cowlick. The word on the street was that Dusty lived down the alley from Ernie and that he was afraid of the ball.

Most people only knew Dusty because he was always making crazy art projects after raiding the neighbors' recycling bins or rescuing Christmas trees from the Dumpster. Dusty was more inclined to haunt hobby shops and garage sales than the hot-seat at the ballpark.

When Swimming Pool had announced her decision to have Dusty as her catcher, Kip had asked, with no small concern, "Um, Dusty. Why Dusty?"

"'Cause I like him," Swimming Pool replied.

Kip was still concerned. "He's afraid of the ball. You know that," he cautioned.

Swimming Pool knew this was probably true. But to her, it didn't matter. "I got my reasons," she said.

Kip didn't fight it. "Okay," he said with resignation, "the job is his."

Even though Swimming Pool had thrown her weight behind landing the job for Dusty, it took some fast talking to actually talk him into it. She knew he'd be attracted to the uniform, of course—the strange-shaped mitt, the metal-grid mask, and the special padding. But apart from that, Dusty really couldn't care less.

"I'm working on peanut butter cookies these days," he explained to Swimming Pool when she came to visit him in the workshop he kept in his parents' toolshed.

"Peanut butter cookies?" Swimming Pool had asked. "Dusty, you can buy peanut butter cookies."

"I want to make them," Dusty said. "Bake them, I mean. I'm looking for the perfect recipe. It's out there and I'm going to find it."

Swimming Pool watched Dusty as his eyes glazed over with a dreamy, faraway look. "Dusty," she said, trying to position herself between Dusty and his quest for the perfect cookie, "you need to get outside. You need fresh air."

Dusty waved his hands as if he couldn't be bothered.

"Look," Swimming Pool argued, "if you play catcher for me, we get to hang out. It'll be fun. Picture it: you at home plate and me on the pitcher's mound. We'll toss the ball around and you can send me secret messages about what pitch to throw."

"Secret messages," Dusty asked. "How do I do that?"

"Hand signals," said Swimming Pool. "Like one finger means fastball and two fingers means curve."

"You mean we get to talk in code?" Dusty asked.

"Well, yeah. It's kind of code, yeah," Swimming Pool said.

Dusty's imagination was already off and running. "Okay, I'm hooked," he said. "Count me in."

In no time at all, Dusty had generated a complicated system of finger-flicks and nose-taps that meant all sorts of different things. Dusty and Swimming Pool had secret word-less conversations that only they could understand. And not always just during the games.

The current Bulldog batter was a stocky kid named Boopie. He was strutting around home plate, tapping his heels with the bat like he knew what he was doing.

"Can we get rid of this kid quick, please?" Dusty asked Swimming Pool with a few tugs on his cap, a flash of three fingers, and a slap on his knee. "He's getting on my nerves."

"Okey-dokey," Swimming Pool responded with the traditional "Okay" sign.

"In fact," Dusty continued, "I think I'm in the mood for a Cincinnati Special." Code for "Cincinnati Special" involved a quick dusting of the plate, a low whistle, and a faraway look at the sky.

Swimming Pool nodded. She signaled another "okey-dokey" and spit for good luck. She checked first base, third base, and then she checked her balance. Twisting to the right, Swimming Pool juiced her arm like she was getting ready to deliver a haymaker, moved through the elaborate steps of her wind-up for the "Cincinnati Special"—a cheer of recognition rose from the stands—and Swimming Pool was just about to release the ball when Ernie started his yodeling routine in the outfield.

"Swim-ming-Pool, Swim-ming-Pool, Swim-ming-Pooooooool!" Ernie sang.

It's hard to say what happened next. Maybe Swimming Pool faltered ever so slightly. Maybe her concentration drifted, just for a moment, to thoughts of Ernie in the outfield—and how they met and how long they'd known each other and all the stuff they'd been through.

Regardless of what was happening in that moment of hesitation, the result was that all the zing in Swimming Pool's "Cincinnati Special" took a sudden and unexpected trip to Miami. Even as the ball left her hand, Swimming Pool gasped. Too late. The ball was gone.

Instead of her secret weapon, Swimming Pool had released the kind of pitch that she usually reserved when she was teaching Brownies not to be afraid of the ball. It was the most candy-coated, gift-wrapped, special-delivery, Valentine's Day sweetheart of a pitch that ever kissed home plate. Swimming Pool listed slightly from one foot to the other and waited for the bad news.

Crack went the bat. Zing went the ball.

And worse than that, it headed for far right field. The ball was headed straight for Ernie.

Back in Outer Mongolia, Ernie had tired of yodeling. He was thinking about baseball—but it wouldn't be accurate to say that Ernie was thinking about the game. In his mind, Ernie was drafting his letter of resignation from baseball. "This whole team manager thing isn't working out," Ernie grumbled to himself.

In the very next moment, Ernie happened to look up to see all the Comets rushing toward him from all corners of the ballpark, flailing their arms, pointing overhead, and shouting incomprehensibly like wildmen.

"What?" cried Ernie. "I didn't do anything! Leave me alone!" And then, of course, Ernie looked up.

It isn't easy to see a baseball in the glare of the sun. Some people say squinting helps. Other people rely on hats or use their hand as a shield. Many people wince into the glare and give up. It is almost impossible to spot a small white ball against the brilliance of the sun.

However, on the rare occasions one gets to glimpse a baseball soaring through the clear blue sky, it can be quite a remarkable thing. A baseball in flight loses the clunky weight it has when it's sitting on the shelf or stuck in some kid's glove. A baseball cresting from one end of the field to the other acquires a new sense of purpose, a sense of freedom and flight. A baseball finds new meaning when it whirls through the air on the thrill of competition and the exhilarating promise of spring. And even though that glowing moment lasts but a brief second before gravity does its thing, a baseball soaring through a clear blue sky can still be a very beautiful sight.

Unless, of course, it's headed for your face.

Swimming Pool was already running toward the outfield when she saw Ernie raise his arms overhead like he was offering the ball a target. Dusty had started running too but he was having difficulty with his padding and the mask.

For a moment, it looked as if Ernie might actually catch the ball. But what they saw next stopped both Swimming Pool and Dusty in their tracks.

Ernie went down like a ton of bricks. Apparently, the baseball had struck Ernie right in the head. It skittered into the grass like a runaway bunny. Several Comets tripped over each other, trying to chase it down.

It was only when Ernie gasped for air that he realized he'd had the wind knocked out of him. And only when his eyes blinked open that he realized he'd been knocked quite solidly off his feet and onto the ground.

Another kid stared down at him, sweaty, wild-eyed, bleary, and a little crazed. Ernie had no idea who it was. Then, a distant voice seemed to travel toward Ernie from the far end of a tunnel. "Ernie, are you okay? Are you okay? Ernie?"

Ernie blinked twice and recognized Ronjon, the kid

who played shortstop. Ernie propped himself on his elbow, and glanced sideways to see Swimming Pool and Dusty running toward him. Beyond them, Mrs. Morgenstern hustled over the diamond with her clipboard and her keys.

Ronjon patted Ernie's shoulder to assure him that he handled difficult situations like this every day. "See?" said Ronjon. "We got you covered. Grown-ups are on their way."

CHAPTER THREE

One Beautiful Shiner

Ernie's face was pressed against a frozen hamburger. "Ow, ow, ow, ow," he moaned dramatically. He sat on a stool, slumped over the kitchen counter with one hand pressed over his bad eye. With his good eye, he watched as Red circled the kitchen, coming closer and closer, until he was right in Ernie's face.

"Lemme see, lemme see," Red urged, pulling Ernie's hand and the hamburger away from the injured eye. Ernie winced in pain, and although he didn't notice it, his father winced slightly too. Ernie tried to be the brave little soldier so he leaned back to give Red the full effect. He squared his shoulders, tilted his head, and raised his chin so that suddenly his black eye was the whole show.

"Well now, that doesn't look so bad," said Red, even though it did.

"This is all your fault," Ernie muttered.

Red placed one hand on Ernie's head and used his fingers to trace the bruises that circled Ernie's eye. Ernie stole a sidelong glance at Red. It had been a long time since he had seen his father's face quite so close. Not since the days of ragged blankets, warm milk, and "night-night."

"Dad," said Ernie, kind of soft and quiet.

"Yes, son," said Red. He was giving the black eye a studious examination.

"There's nothing we can't talk about, right?" Ernie asked.

"Of course," said Red. "What's on your mind?"

"You need to clip the hairs in your nose," Ernie replied.

Red made as if to whack the back of Ernie's head, then he smiled broadly and said with gusto, "I'll tell you what. That is one beautiful shiner!"

"Dad!" Ernie snarled, and slapped the hamburger back over his eye.

"Whoa, whoa, not so fast," said Red. "Hand over the hamburger." Red already had a grip on the package. He swapped the hamburger for a bag of frozen corn that he pressed into Ernie's hand and closed like a compress against his face.

"Ow! Be gentle," Ernie moaned. "How come you can't be gentle?"

Red didn't answer. Instead, he reached for the bookshelf over the cutting board and pulled down the Home Medical Encyclopedia. He flipped to the section on "black eyes" and slid the book in front of Ernie. "Here," said Red. "Read."

"I can't read," Ernie protested. "I'm blind! I got a black eye!"

"Read with your good eye," said Red.

Ernie slumped over the Home Medical Encyclopedia and began to read aloud, using a phony authoritative voice like the experts on the medical channel. "A black eye occurs in response to trauma," Ernie intoned. "The tissue around the eye responds to injury with redness, swelling, and resultant pain—or, as it is known in Latin, the—"

"Skip the Latin," said Red, "and cut to the chase." He tossed the hamburger into the microwave and set the dial to defrost.

Ernie skipped down the paragraph until he found a sentence of substance. "Although the response to trauma results in pain and a black and swollen eye—," Ernie began, pausing momentarily to point at his own injured eye before continuing, "the result of the response is healing of the injury which is ultimately beneficial to the eye."

"'Ultimately beneficial,'" repeated Red. "So it gets better, see?"

"I dunno," said Ernie as he closed the book and chucked it aside. "All I'm reading is pain, pain, pain." He pressed the frozen corn to his head like it was a baby blanket and he needed comfort.

Red jerked open the freezer and grabbed another frozen package. He held it toward Ernie. "Swap blueberries for corn," said Red, doing the gimme-gimme with his hand. "I'm not going to be baking a blueberry pie anytime soon."

They tossed the bags and did a midair swap. Ernie placed the frozen blueberries flat on the counter and pressed his head against it. Red poured the corn into a pot of boiling water. He turned to look at Ernie, perched on the stool with his head pressed against the bag of blueberries. "You know," Red ventured, "I think this black eye might be good for you."

Ernie moaned. "Good for me how?" he asked, in a tone that suggested that the answer was unimaginable.

"It'll toughen you up," said Red.

"Your cooking toughens me up plenty," said Ernie, resting his head back down on the blueberries.

"Ha, ha, funny, funny," said Red. He looked at the clock, grimaced, and braced himself against the countertop. "I was supposed to meet the guys from the plant to catch a game on TV but now I think I shouldn't go," said Red.

"Dad, go watch the game," Ernie urged. "You need friends, you know that. We talked about this."

"Yeah, but I can't leave you alone with this big black eye. What if you have a concussion?" said Red.

"A concussion?" asked Ernie, suddenly alarmed. "What's a concussion?"

Red shoved the encyclopedia back down the counter and said, "Look it up."

At that moment, there was a knock at the kitchen door. Red threw a curious look at Ernie that meant, "Are you expecting anybody?" Ernie shrugged his shoulders as if to say, "I'm not expecting anybody."

Red opened the kitchen door to find Swimming Pool standing on the back porch. She must have just dropped her bike at the bottom of the stairs because the wheels were still spinning.

"Swimming Pool!" said Red. "Did you stop by to check on the new team manager?"

"Yeah, how's the patient?" Swimming Pool asked. She

entered the kitchen and closed the door behind her.

"Cranky," said Red. "Nice of you to stop by, Swimming Pool." Red gave her a conspiratorial wink because, in truth, Ernie's stint as team manager had been Swimming Pool's idea in the first place. Swimming Pool gave Red a look that said he should zip it.

"Least I could do," she replied brightly. "Hey, Ernie, brought you something." She held a brown paper bag.

"Hey, Pool," Ernie said. He lowered his head back onto the blueberries, retreating into his pain, and issued a miserable grunt.

Red looked at Ernie and Swimming Pool together and smiled knowingly. He clapped his hands and rubbed them briskly like he was starting a fire. "Okay, then," he said brightly. "Hamburger defrosting and corn on the boil! Oh, I'm a good cook!" Red plucked a newspaper off the counter and jerked his thumb toward the next room. "Dinner should be ready in twenty minutes," he said with an odd amount of delight, "but until then—maybe I should leave you two alone!" He had a silly grin on his face.

Swimming Pool and Ernie both watched as Red backed out of the room and into the hall.

"What's his problem?" said Swimming Pool.

"Beats me," muttered Ernie, his voice buried in blueberries.

"Parents," said Swimming Pool, rolling her eyes. She circled the kitchen until she reached Ernie. "Did Dusty drop by?" she asked.

"Yeah," said Ernie. "He brought me a bag of peanut butter cookies."

Swimming Pool nodded. "And how were they?" she

asked, like she already knew the answer.

"Excellent," Ernie responded, "although not quite perfect enough for Dusty."

Ernie appreciated Dusty's cookies but, as he recalled, the visit had been a little strange. Dusty handed over the cookies and hopped onto the kitchen counter without a word. He watched as Ernie wolfed down the whole bag and all he did was stare at Ernie's eye. It was like Dusty was mesmerized by the injury. Finally, Ernie said, "Get outta here, Dusty, you're creeping me out!" And Dusty went home.

"Is the Dust-man okay?" Ernie asked Swimming Pool.

"I think something's going on," said Swimming Pool, and they left it at that. Swimming Pool pushed the brown paper bag in front of Ernie and said, "Surprise!"

"What's this?" Ernie asked. He reached into the bag and pulled out an old-fashioned ice pack. It was a mound of pleated tartan plaid that looked like a big Scottish cream puff.

"It's a family heirloom," Swimming Pool explained. "There's a white cap that unscrews on top." She twisted the cap so that Ernie could see the empty cavity inside. "The ice goes there. Then you perch the whole thing on your head."

"Thanks," said Ernie.

"I thought you'd appreciate it," said Swimming Pool. She grabbed the frozen blueberries to return them to the freezer. Once there, she stood with the freezer door open and peered at the shelves. "Ice cubes?" Swimming Pool asked.

"Good luck," said Ernie. The prospect was unlikely. Swimming Pool poked among the ice-cube trays saying "Ice? No dice," over and over again. Ernie dangled the ice pack and peered curiously at it from all sides. "Where'd this thing come from?" he asked.

"Belonged to my dad in high school football," Swimming Pool explained. "It's been around. It's a big deal in my family. You have to ask permission to get Mom to haul it down from the cupboard over the sink."

"I hope you didn't go to any trouble," said Ernie.

"No, no, no bother," said Swimming Pool. "We always ask for it whenever somebody's got a sprain or a break or a concussion or a headache or maybe a black eye. Mom likes to keep track of which brother got injured doing what."

Ernie laughed a bit even though it hurt. Swimming Pool was the only girl in a family of six brothers. "This ice pack has been through a lot," he said.

"I know," said Swimming Pool. "Pretty funny, huh."

Swimming Pool tugged on another ice tray and hit pay-dirt. "Eureka!" she cried, displaying the tray and crossing back to the counter. She placed the tray in front of Ernie so that they could pluck ice cubes, one by one, and drop them into the ice pack.

Swimming Pool had hoped to bring up the subject of baseball while Ernie was preoccupied in a completely different task altogether. This seemed like a good time.

"So, Ernie," she said, "the whole baseball team manager thing? That working out for you?"

"I hate it," Ernie groused. "I'm gonna resign."

"Don't resign," said Swimming Pool. "You'd make a great team manager. The team needs you."

Ernie went deadpan. "News to me," he said. "Do you know how many Comets said they were sorry about my black eye? None." Ernie snorted and looked away.

"That's not true," said Swimming Pool. "Ronjon stayed with you the whole time."

"Ronjon doesn't even know my name," said Ernie. "I'm just the kid in Outer Mongolia."

"Ernie," she said sternly, "Ronjon helped Dusty and me and Mrs. Morgenstern carry you off the field."

"Thank you, Ronjon," Ernie said grudgingly, "but I didn't see Kip lifting a finger, did I?"

Swimming Pool winced slightly. She thought it best not to comment on the tension between Ernie and Kip. Swimming Pool had taken a deliberate backseat when Ernie showed up on the Comets' playing field. She figured Ernie needed to make friends on his own. Still, she was convinced that Ernie needed the Comets as much as the Comets needed Ernie.

"Look," said Swimming Pool. "Don't quit. I really don't want you to quit."

"For the life of me, I cannot imagine why," said Ernie. "I'm no use to that team at all." By this point, the ice pack was bulging at the seams.

"Ernie, if you must know, you are," said Swimming Pool.

"Then what am I doing in Outer Mongolia?" asked Ernie. "Admit it, Pool, I'm not the sporty type. I'm an idea man. A brainstormer. I'd be a total brainiac if I made better grades." He tried to screw the white cap back onto the ice pack but he wasn't seeing too well so Swimming Pool took charge.

"And a brainiac is precisely what we need on the team," Swimming Pool concluded. "The Comets get distracted by the scores and the stats. The business stuff never gets done.

We need you, Ernie. I'm not saying you won't have to assert yourself and Mrs. Morgenstern is always changing the rules, but I really think we need you on the team."

Ernie was quiet. Already the wheels were turning. "So," he said, "you guys are thinking of getting rid of Mrs. Morgenstern?"

"We don't have to," said Swimming Pool. "Mr. O'Malley takes over next week anyway." She checked the seal on the ice pack and tossed it into the air. Ice cubes jiggered and jostled inside.

"Isn't that interesting?" said Ernie. "No Mrs. Morgenstern. What's the word on O'Malley?"

"Beats me," Pool responded. "Coaches come, coaches go." Swimming Pool lifted the ice pack overhead and gestured toward Ernie. "Nudge over," she said. Ernie shifted until he was situated beneath it. Swimming Pool let go of the bag and it settled onto his head like a lopsided crown.

"There," Swimming Pool said, with a slight lilt to her voice. "Now you're beautiful."

"How bad is a black eye?" Ernie asked.

Swimming Pool pulled a face. "Don't worry about it," she said. "I've had plenty. My life has been a series of door-knobs and tether balls and dogpiles and bullies."

"Doorknobs?" Ernie asked incredulously.

"Don't ask," said Swimming Pool. She shoved away from the counter and crumpled the brown paper bag. "I gotta be more careful. I think my mom's getting a little sick of me coming home all bruised up and stuff."

"What do you mean?" asked Ernie.

"She was acting weird when I asked for the ice pack,"

she said with annoyance. "I go, 'Can I have the ice pack?' And Mom goes, 'What now?'" Swimming Pool put her hands on her hips and made her mom sound irritable and nasty.

"Doesn't sound so bad to me," said Ernie.

"Maybe it's not what she said but the way she said it," Swimming Pool responded. "I mean, she gave me the ice pack, but she was checking for damage. I told her about your black eye and she calmed down."

"That's good," said Ernie.

"Yeah, but still," Swimming Pool agreed, somewhat halfheartedly. "You know, *parents*." She emphasized the word like it was the title of a horror movie.

Ernie laughed. "You make them sound so scary."

"Well, they are scary," said Swimming Pool. "I'm serious. You never know what they're up to." She pushed away from the counter and headed for the kitchen door. "All I did was ask for the ice pack. I can just hear it now. I'll get home and Mom will have talked to Dad and the whole deal will have turned into some big weird thing."

She grabbed the doorknob and gave it a tug.

"Hey, thanks for the ice pack," said Ernie. He got off the stool so that he could show Swimming Pool to the door but by the time he turned around so that he could actually use his good eye, Swimming Pool was already gone.

CHAPTER FOUR

Some Big Weird Thing

It wasn't much of a ballpark. The chain-link fencing was rusty and falling apart. The asphalt parking lot was a field of potholes. The fourth row of the bleachers was missing in action. On the far side of home plate, which was already cracked, the baseball diamond had been fairly trampled and the wooden wall that skirted the outfield was missing so many planks that it looked like the smile of a six-year-old kid after a visit from the Tooth Fairy. The grass was patchy. The old scoreboard had never been replaced. "Yes, yes, a bee-yoo-tee-ful day for a ball game!" the announcer would crow through a pair of broken speakers, but the message never seemed to suit the ballpark.

After a few days, when Ernie's eye was a little less disgusting, he showed up one day at the ballpark on schedule for the Comets' practice. To his surprise, the playing field was empty. "This is weird," Ernie thought. He approached the dugout to find Dusty holding court outside with a gaggle of sweaty Comets. The boys were making the disgusted yet impressed sounds boys make in the presence of something gross.

Ernie tapped Dusty on the shoulder. "What's going on?" he said.

Dusty turned around and gave Ernie the shock of his young life. Dusty had a horrifically grisly black eye. "Dusty! What happened to you?" Ernie cried.

"It's ink!" Dusty said with a certain pride.

The gaggle of Comets all laughed.

"Doesn't it look real?" said Noah, a little boy with a crew cut and freckles.

Ernie pulled Dusty aside. "What is going on with you?" he asked.

"Ernie, I couldn't stop thinking about your black eye," Dusty said. "I even dreamed about it. When I woke up, I went to brush my teeth and lo and behold, there was a black marker by the sink." Dusty shrugged. "I took it as a sign," he said, swiveling his head from side to side to show off his creation. "*Voilà!* Instant black eye! Isn't it great?"

"So cool!" cried Noah. "I want one!" A chorus of boys chimed "Me too!" not to be outdone. Dusty lifted his black eye toward Ernie and winked.

"I don't think this is so funny," said Ernie, heading for the dugout.

Dusty called out after him. "It's not supposed to be funny," he cried. "It's art! It's an homage!"

But Ernie wasn't interested. "Great," Ernie thought to himself. "I can't even have a black eye without getting upstaged by Dusty."

Ernie stepped into the dugout and entered a total madhouse. Kip was engaged in an intense staring contest with Larry, a slightly cross-eyed kid with glasses. Ronjon was comparing knee scabs with Marcus. Another kid was prying strings of bubble gum from the sole of his shoe while two other boys counted through a mind-numbingly endless exchange of knuckle sandwiches.

"No Swimming Pool," Ernie thought. But that was typical. Swimming Pool was always late.

Ernie worked up the nerve to interrupt Kip in the middle of his staring contest. Kip was seated opposite Larry, the notorious dugout-staring-contest champion, and it was an intense match. Larry sat with his characteristic quiet bemusement like a Buddha while Kip appeared to be sweating bullets.

"O Captain, my Captain," Ernie said to Kip, with forced congeniality. "I hate to interrupt but aren't we supposed to be in the middle of practice?"

"Talk-to-Mr.-O'Malley," said Kip in a rush, keeping his focus on Larry.

"O-kay," said Ernie. "Where's Mr. O'Malley?"

"Sitting-on-the-hood-of-his-car-screaming-at-Mrs.-Morgenstern," Kip answered. The words came out in a flurry so Ernie would get the message that Kip didn't want to be talking right now. Ernie glanced through the chain-link fence and, sure enough, there was Mr. O'Malley perched on his car beside the playing field. He was barking into his cell phone and gesticulating wildly so that Ernie automatically knew that something was wrong. "So what's the problem?" Ernie asked, interrupting the staring contest once more.

This time Larry spoke. He made his voice sound flat, even, and direct like a computer. Without shifting his gaze from Kip, he said, "Mrs. Morgenstern forgot to give the equipment duffel to Mr. O'Malley. It's still in the trunk of her car and Mr. O'Malley is stuck coaching fifteen kids with no balls, no bats, no gloves, and no whistles."

This was bad. "So no equipment, no practice?" Ernie surmised. Kip shrugged and did not answer.

"Or are we supposed to wait and see if practice happens?" Ernie asked. Still Kip offered no answer.

Ernie tried a different approach. "My black eye still hurts," he said. "Does anybody care?" Still no answer.

Ernie didn't appreciate the cold shoulder. Ever since he'd offered his services as team manager, all he had gotten from Kip was the cold shoulder. He observed the chaos around him and weighed his options. Half of him wanted to take his black eye and go home. The other half reminded him of what Swimming Pool had said: "You might have to assert yourself, Ernie." Maybe he would.

"Although," said Ernie, dragging out the word as the idea dawned on him, "we could take advantage of the time and hold an official Comets business meeting."

Kip flinched but held his focus. "An official meeting? About what?"

Ernie knew he was dropping a bomb, but he dropped it anyway. "This team is a disaster," he said. "At least that's what I heard."

Kip balked and broke his eye contact with Larry. "I did it! I win, I win!" cried Larry, goofy, giddy, and clearly over-invested in his staring-contest title.

Kip was intent on Ernie. "Who says this team is a disaster?" he asked hotly, jabbing his finger at Ernie's chest. "Are you bad-mouthing the Comets?" Kip raised his voice so that the whole team could hear.

"Uh-oh," thought Ernie. A low rumble ran across the dugout and the team fell silent. Ernie and Kip were having a showdown.

Dusty pushed into the dugout but there were too many Comets in the way and none of them would budge.

Ernie couldn't believe what was happening. "Isn't this ironic?" he thought. "I finally get attention from the Comets when I'm about to be pummeled."

Ernie didn't think Kip really wanted to fight. Ernie had almost been in fights before so he used the same strategy he always used. He took the moral high ground and tried to play for a laugh.

"Get real, Kip," said Ernie. "Go ahead and hit me. I already took one black eye for this team."

"Two would make a raccoon," said Ronjon. It was a lame joke but it generated enough laughs to break the tension. Ronjon smiled at Ernie as if to say, "You owe me one."

When the laughter died down, Ernie took charge. "I'm not saying anything bad about the Comets," he declared, stepping onto the bench for all the Comets to hear. "All I'm saying is that if the Comets had a real team manager, the team manager could be in charge of the equipment and then the equipment could be at the playing field and then the Comets could actually practice."

It was quiet in the dugout. Nobody knew what was going to happen. Then a voice at the far end of the dugout said, "Hear, hear."

"Who said that?" said Kip. "Speak up."

The Comets parted. Ernie watched as Dusty rose from the crowd and stood on the bench. "Hear, hear," he said again. "I think Ernie has a good idea."

Kip pursed his lips and nodded as if maybe Ernie was right. "Okay," he said, "point taken. But I gotta ask. If we need a team manager to manage the equipment, what do we do with the batboy?"

Noah, the freckle-faced kid with the crew cut, waved his hand and shouted, "Me! I'm batboy! I already got elected!" Several Comets rolled their eyes. That election had happened during Mrs. Morgenstern's reign and Noah happened to be Mrs. Morgenstern's son.

Ernie smiled smugly. Kip was playing hardball. "Okey-dokey," he thought. "If Kip wants to play hardball, hardball it is."

"Fair enough, Kip," he said. "You're the team captain. What do you think the team manager should do?" He spread his palms generously to convey that he was willing to entertain any suggestions.

To Ernie's surprise, Kip had actually given the matter some thought. "Well," he said, "it would be ideal if we had a team manager who could do something about this ballpark."

There was a chorus of agreement from the Comets.

"Fix the ballpark," they cried. "This place is a dump!"

"A bee-yoo-tee-ful day for a ball game!" several Comets crowed, imitating the corny voice on the loudspeakers.

"I like the dump," said Ronjon, but he was quickly shouted down by the other Comets.

Ernie couldn't believe his ears. "Fix the ballpark? You gotta be kidding me," he said. "How am I supposed to fix this dump?"

"So we agree there's a problem," said Kip, "but you don't intend to do anything about it."

Ernie narrowed his eyes. Kip had just walked him into a trap. Ernie didn't have a clue about how to fix the ballpark. His jaw dropped ever so slightly, but enough to let Kip know that he had won the showdown.

"I thought so," Kip said with a smirk. He straddled the bench to challenge Larry to another staring contest. "Come on, Four Eyes," he said, "what do you say two out of three?"

Ernie felt completely defeated. He'd been humiliated as team manager. There was no point in asserting himself anymore. Kip had just made a fool of him and he might as well go home.

At that very moment, a sudden crash and a loud bang rattled the dugout. All the boys jumped.

They looked up to find Swimming Pool clinging to the chain link overhead. Her face was pressed against the grid.

"What's up, Pool?" said Kip.

Swimming Pool twisted her mouth in anger. "Calamity! Ruination! Disaster!" she barked, then she threw herself over the side.

The Comets craned their necks to track Swimming Pool as she stalked the exterior of the dugout. "What's going on?" they cried. "What's the matter with you?"

Swimming Pool huffed and puffed a few times and then spit the words out. "Mom says I can't play baseball anymore!" she cried. "Mom says I have to quit the team!"

The Comets let out a roar of disapproval. "Quit the Comets?" cried Kip, as though his life was falling apart. "But why?"

Swimming Pool flung herself into the dugout, hanging onto the top railing, ready for pull-ups. "Mom logic!" cried Swimming Pool. "That's my curse!"

"Wait a minute," Ernie blustered. Everyone was getting carried away over nothing. "Swimming Pool, calm down! Just tell us what's going on!"

Swimming Pool flung herself face first over the bench like she'd just been shot. Her voice sounded crushed. "Mom says girls aren't supposed to play rough. Mom says girls have to be 'pretty.' And 'nice.'" She punched her mom's words to make them sound all the more ridiculous.

There was a flurry of debate among the Comets as to whether girls could play rough and whether all girls were pretty. "Plenty of girls play sports!" Kip blustered.

"Oh, sure," said Swimming Pool. "But apparently I don't get to be one of them anymore. I have to be a nice, sweet girlie-girl for my mom."

The dugout exploded with a flurry of outrage. Swimming Pool waved her hands to hold the peace. "And it gets worse," she said.

The team sat in disbelief. "Worse?" cried Kip. "What could be worse than what we've already heard?"

Swimming Pool tried to break the news as delicately as possible. "Mom says no Little League," she said, "and no birthday party, either!"

A second explosion rocked the dugout. Swimming Pool was the uncontested queen of birthdays. Her parties were legendary. Three years ago was the bowling alley, two years ago was go-carts, and last year was the wax museum. Actually, the wax museum was a bit of a bust, but otherwise Swimming Pool's parties had a consistent reputation for excellence. There was always lots of anticipation concerning next year's birthday surprise.

Ernie was a relatively new friend so he was still a stranger to Swimming Pool's parties. The extreme dismay of the Comets caught him by surprise. Kip was cradling his head, Larry rattled the chain link, and Ronjon shook his fists at the skies. "Your mom is too mean!" cried Ronjon.

"Cruel and unusual," said Kip.

Again, Ernie tried to be the peacemaker. "Pool, isn't there anything we can do?" he said.

Swimming Pool shook her head like it was an impossible situation. "There is one thing," she said, "but it's so ridiculous that it's out of the question."

The boys murmured among themselves. "What? What is it?" they cried.

Swimming Pool sighed heavily. "You're not going to believe it," she said. "Mom has this crazy idea of sending me to charm school!"

The Comets stared blankly at Swimming Pool. Not a word was said. Swimming Pool had expected the news to draw the same explosion of rage that had already visited the dugout but, instead, everything got quiet. Too quiet.

"Charm school!" she scoffed. "Can you believe it?"

"Yeah, we heard you," muttered Ronjon. Otherwise, she could have heard a pin drop.

Swimming Pool stepped onto the bench to grandstand how ridiculous the charm school idea was. "Mom thinks I need to learn manners and girlie stuff and learn how to dance. She wants me to act all ladylike!" Swimming Pool tiptoed in her sneakers like she was prancing in high heels.

"My sister learned to curtsy," said Chuck.

"They serve punch," said Ronjon. "And cookies, too."

Swimming Pool glared at him. "How do you know that?"

"My sisters went," said Ronjon.

"We're getting off the subject," said Ernie. "Let's stick with the bottom line." He turned toward Swimming Pool. "So what'd you tell your mom?"

"I told her to forget it!" said Swimming Pool. She threw her hands on her hips to re-create the showdown with her mother. It was a much greater display of defiance than Swimming Pool had actually shown, but it made for a better story. "I told her," Swimming Pool snarled, "that I didn't need baseball or a birthday party and she couldn't force me to go to charm school, no way, no how! I am n-o-t 'not' going to Charm School!"

The dugout was already hushed but it slid into a suspicious quietude. The kind that suggests that everyone has an opinion but they're keeping their mouths shut.

Swimming Pool eyed the boys. "Wha-aat?" she muttered, slightly miffed. Her eyes traveled from one boy to the next. Ernie shifted his attention to a far corner of the sky as if he had just caught a glimpse of Halley's Comet. Dusty pursed his lips to whistle a little song that didn't have a tune. Kip found a knot in his shoelaces that required surgical repair. Larry had his finger up his nose. And Ronjon, never without something to say, flexed his lips pensively four or five different ways.

"Okay, wha-at?" Swimming Pool repeated. "What's going on? What?"

The boys stirred but no one spoke.

"It's nothing," Kip ventured. "Nothing. Just such a shame." He was almost on the verge of tears. "What can I say?" Kip was really losing it.

Swimming Pool shot her eyes at Ernie. "'Fess up, Ernie," she said. "I'm counting on you for the truth."

All eyes turned to Ernie. It was a unique moment in the dugout. Ernie felt like a spotlight had just clicked on. He lifted his shoulders to shrug, but then he sighed a little and said, quite simply, "Swimming Pool, what's charm school?"

"What is charm school?" Dusty echoed. He honestly didn't know the answer but the idea of punch and cookies sounded pretty good.

"My point exactly," Ernie continued. "Dusty and I are in perfect sync. What's charm school? What's a curtsy?"

"It's a little bow that girls do with their dresses," said Noah, but Ernie cut him off.

"It's not like charm school is detention, is it?" Ernie said, looking over at the boys for reassurance. Several boys nodded even though they weren't sure why.

"Ugh," Swimming Pool snarled. "If charm school sounds like so much fun, why don't *you* go?"

Ernie spread his palms. He had nothing to hide. "Nobody asked me," he said, "but if they did, I'd have to ask myself—"

"Ask yourself what?" said Swimming Pool.

Ernie shrugged. He didn't want to lay it on too thick. "Swimming Pool," he said, "all I'm saying is—what's a curtsy—next to the good of the team?"

A murmur of appreciation passed over the dugout. "The good of the team" was an unbeatable argument in baseball. "Do it for the team, Swimming Pool," Kip urged, just about ready to cry. "Swimming Pool, you *are* this team!"

Swimming Pool crossed her arms and curled her lip. "I am *not* going to charm school! This is not fair! You guys are setting me up!"

"Oh, it's your decision, Pool," Ernie interrupted in his best, even-tempered, Sunday-morning voice. "And whatever you decide, we're behind you 100 percent." Then, unexpectedly, Ernie cocked his head and looked at Swimming Pool as though he was seeing her for the first time. "But I have to say," he continued, "I am surprised."

"Surprised at what?" Swimming Pool asked, with no small annoyance.

"You love baseball," Ernie said in a tone that was gracious and sad. "I would have thought you'd have jumped at the chance to make a sacrifice for your team."

A second murmur of appreciation passed over the dugout. In the realm of Comets' baseball, "sacrifice" was a magic word and Ronjon was the expert.

Last season, Ronjon was next at bat when the game was two outs with a runner on third. It was also the only game in the entire season that Ronjon's parents had been able to attend. Ronjon had the choice of showing off for his parents or sacrificing himself at bat to bring the runner in. Ronjon made the sacrifice, got tagged out, and the entire team carried him off the field in a grand show of appreciation. Ronjon still glowed at the memory.

Swimming Pool was almost afraid to make eye contact with Ronjon and when she did, she found that he was already looking at her with his best puppy-dog eyes.

"Do it, Swimming Pool," said Ronjon with feeling. "You'll feel better, I know."

Swimming Pool threw a look at Ernie and pushed her way through the boys. No one said anything. They stepped aside to give her plenty of room. When she reached the entrance to the dugout, Swimming Pool whirled about to face the team.

"Okay, I'll do it," Swimming Pool said with quiet intensity. Nobody dared cheer. "But I am telling you one thing," she added. Swimming Pool let her eyes travel over the team, making eye contact with each Comet, including a significant glance at Ernie. She clenched a fist tightly as she issued a vow. "I am not going to wear another ding-dang dress!"

After Swimming Pool's bicycle had cleared the field, the boys in the dugout burst into applause. Boys who couldn't even remember Ernie's name grabbed him for handshakes and high-fives. Ernie was overwhelmed.

Dusty worked himself into a wedge beside Ernie and tugged on his shirt. "Ernie, Ernie," Dusty asked in a frantic voice, "is Swimming Pool going to be okay?"

"She'll be okay," said Ernie. "Don't worry about it."

"Sure," said Dusty. "She'll be okay. After all, there's punch and cookies, right?"

Dusty was interrupted by the arrival of Kip. He wrapped an arm around Ernie and gave him a significant smile. "Good job, Team Manager," Kip said.

"Team manager," said Ernie, bursting with pride. "That's got an awful nice ring to it."

CHAPTER FIVE

Another Ding-Dang Dress

It took more than two hours at the Shop-and-Save for Swimming Pool and her mother to agree on another ding-dang dress for charm school. Swimming Pool eventually settled on a blue job that didn't have too much fuss and bother.

Swimming Pool hadn't anticipated how excited her mother would be by the dress-selection process. Once they hit the girls department, her mother started grabbing hangers right and left, off the clearance rack and the fancy racks too. Swimming Pool insisted that she could not endure the pain but her mother was determined. They ended up in the dressing room with armfuls of the worst frilly offenses.

Swimming Pool's mother flipped through the hangers chirping, "Oh, look!" like each dress was a new discovery. For Swimming Pool, of course, each dress was a new indictment.

She gaped and groaned, "Ooof! Ugh! Yowie!" like a cartoon superhero battling the cosmos.

Eventually, Swimming Pool's mom held up a frilly job with yellow buttons and bows. Swimming Pool lost it altogether. She growled through her teeth and cried, "You're killing me, Ma!" She didn't care if the entire dressing room could hear. Swimming Pool was on the verge of real tears when her mother cried, "Enough!"

Swimming Pool's mother scooped up the dresses and swept out of the changing room. For a moment, Swimming Pool thought she had been spared. Unfortunately, her mother returned an instant later with a second wave of even more outrageous dresses.

"Mom!" Swimming Pool groaned. "I thought we were done!"

"No, no, no," her mother explained. "The dressing room only permits eight dresses at a time. We've only just begun!"

Swimming Pool's mom was on a mission.

Fortunately, Swimming Pool had a secret weapon. She had taken the time beforehand to sit down with Ernie and come up with a strategy. They had each arranged for hallway passes during fourth period and met in the computer room of the library.

"Did you bring the list?" Ernie asked.

"Got it right here," she said, tapping her head.

Ernie grimaced. "It's not a real list unless you write it down," he said, opening a notebook and ripping out a sheet of paper. "Let's have it. A list of all the things you're not willing to negotiate."

"I remember," said Swimming Pool. She bent over the paper with a pen and announced her items as she wrote them down. "Anything-pink," she declared, slowing her speech so that it kept pace with her handwriting, "anything-goofy, and anything-with-ribbons."

Ernie leaned forward to study the list and ask Swimming Pool about the intensity of her feelings. He wanted to give Swimming Pool a chance to blow off some steam.

When Swimming Pool had ranted enough, Ernie took the list and folded it up. He tapped it against his lips as he gave the matter careful consideration.

Swimming Pool turned her chair around so that she was straddling it backward. "All right already," she said impatiently. "What do you think?"

After a slight pause, Ernie said one word: "Sleeves."

"Sleeves?" Swimming Pool grunted. Ernie hadn't been listening at all. "I don't care about sleeves," she cried. "I care about pink and goofy and anything-with-ribbons!"

"My point exactly," Ernie responded. "Trust me, Pool, you have to pick one item that's a total deal-breaker. Something that will absolutely make you hold your breath and turn blue."

"But I don't care about sleeves!" Swimming Pool repeated.

"I know you don't," Ernie answered, reassuringly. "Who would? Who cares about sleeves?" He leaned forward to emphasize his next point. "The deal-breaker is always something totally who-cares!"

Swimming Pool looked more confused than ever. Ernie unfolded the note and pointed to the words. "If sleeves are the deal-breaker," he concluded, "your mom is going to give up on anything-pink, anything-goofy, and anything-with-ribbons. She'll be happy if she gets you in a dress at all!"

"Ohhhh," Swimming Pool said, finally catching on.

"See what I mean?" Ernie continued. "Win on the other stuff and who cares if you end up with sleeves?"

As it turned out, this was excellent advice.

In the dressing room, Swimming Pool's mother was getting all moony over a total cupcake of a dress. It was the worst offender yet. Pink, goofy, and riddled with ribbons. It also happened to have a page-boy collar and distinctively puffy sleeves. For a moment, Swimming Pool thought her mother had completely lost her mind. Then Swimming Pool saw the smile on her mother's face and she realized that her mother was serious. Swimming Pool practically had to go ballistic on the linoleum in order to avoid that disaster. "No, no, no!" she cried, gritting her teeth as she turned up the volume.

"I just don't see what's the matter with it," her mother insisted.

Swimming Pool had a trademark wail that sounded a lot like a Tarzan yell and she was just about to use it when she remembered Ernie's advice. "It has sleeves!" she cried. "I said no sleeves! You promised! No sleeves!"

"All right, already!" her mother conceded. "No sleeves!"

Swimming Pool's mother snatched the remaining dresses and fumed quietly as she waited for Swimming Pool to change back into her overalls. She leaned against the door to the changing room and almost whispered, "I don't know where you got your temper from. It certainly wasn't from me!"

With the battle won, Swimming Pool calmed right down. She buttoned her overalls and was just about to reach for her red high tops when she paused to comment, "Say, what's this?" She raised the simple blue job that was lost beneath the heap of dresses. "What's this dress doing down there?" she asked innocently.

Swimming Pool held the dress in the mirror and looked at it from side to side. "It's simple and blue," she observed. "Not too complicated."

Swimming Pool's mother looked disappointed but relieved and resigned. They returned the other dresses to the rack and Swimming Pool carried the simple blue job that she had spotted from the start directly to the cashier's lane.

The ding-dang dress in question was as straightforward as they come, except for the fact that it had a little duck stitched along the fabric at the hem. In truth, Swimming Pool thought that the little duck was the best part of the dress but she tried to act like she hadn't even noticed it was there at all.

Swimming Pool's mother pulled out a disposable camera when Swimming Pool was forced to model the dress after supper. Swimming Pool put up a protest but her father started talking about the value of a dollar and it was easier to wear the dress than to listen to that lecture again. Swimming Pool's mother warned that if the brothers started laughing like hyenas, they'd be banished from the room. Swimming Pool's father banished them anyway just to avoid the fight.

When Swimming Pool entered the room, her father

pushed his chair away from the table so that he could get a good look. Swimming Pool still didn't feel safe. Whenever her mother's camera flashed, Swimming Pool crossed her eyes, stuck out her tongue or pulled the skirt over her head.

"I like the duck," Swimming Pool's father said. "Where?" Swimming Pool asked with alarm, pretending that the news was a complete surprise. She hitched up her skirt and scrutinized the hem like she was searching for a stain. "What duck?" she asked incredulously, turning round and round like a dog chasing its tail.

"There, no, there!" her father said, pointing, until finally there was no escaping the fact of the duck.

"Oh, great," Swimming Pool muttered with disgust. "A duck." She threw the skirt down in disgust. Her life had reached a new low. "Quack, quack."

"The duck is my favorite part," her father said. Swimming Pool looked like she was in pain but she still stepped forward with her skirt extended to share the duck with her dad.

CHAPTER SIX

Tuna Surprise

Already the Comets were changing.

Some of the adjustments were obvious, like the stacking order on the bike rack. "O Captain, my Captain," Ernie said to Kip, "can't we do something about the bike rack? It's hard enough running the organization without having to leave our bicycles in a heap!"

"What do you suggest, Team Manager?" asked Kip.

The first change of the new administration was to assign slots on the bike rack so that Team Captain and Team Manager had the prime spots, just across from the dugout and right next to the water fountain. "You gotta love the perks!" Ernie said with a smile as he secured his bike on a brand-new day at the ballpark.

Another obvious change was the fact that Ernie wasn't

playing far right outfield anymore. No one was surprised in the least when Ernie retired to the position of dugout consultant and turned in his glove. To fill the outfield post, Ernie and Kip decided to promote the batboy and give him what had been Ernie's glove.

"Hoo-hoo," cried Noah Morgenstern, trotting off to Outer Mongolia. "Look at me! Look at me now!"

Other changes weren't quite so obvious. For example, the Comets finally started showing up on time after Ernie instituted a call sheet with all the carpool parents' cell phone numbers and started charging them a dollar late fee during practice. "Hit 'em in their wallet," Ernie told Kip. "Works every time."

Ernie was also determined to get the Comets onto the field without too much horsing around. He and Kip stood on the third base line and kept a watchful eye for goofing off during practice. If they spotted any shenanigans, they launched into a private conversation at the top of their lungs.

"Say Kip," barked Ernie, "do you think the Army Girls are horsing around?"

"Why no, Ernie," Kip called in response, "I don't!"

"What about the Baldwinsville Cubs or the Solvay Tigers?" Ernie continued. "Are they horsing around?"

"No," shouted Kip, "I would bet they are not!"

"Gee," said Ernie, still real loud, "why do you think that is?"

"I'll tell you why, Ernie," said Kip, delivering the kicker and getting louder still, "because they want to win ball games!"

After they dropped the hammer, Ernie and Kip would

always offer motivational encouragement like "Run faster!" "Jump higher!" and "Go for it, go for it, go for it!" It sounds silly but the positive encouragement really seemed to help.

After practice, Ernie slugged up the back steps of his brown-stone and clomped his heels against the top step to clear the dirt off his cleats. He reached for the key under the rock and let himself in through the back door.

It was already dark inside and Ernie couldn't find the light switch. "Oh well," he thought, stepping inside.

"Hello, Ernie!" a voice said.

Ernie almost jumped out of his skin. He let out a whoop and tumbled backward. His heels did the Mexican Hat Dance while his hands did the Macarena. His legs did the Argentine tango, his hips did a little belly dance and his knees did the Irish jig. It would have carried on like "Dances of Many Nations" except one of Ernie's cleats got stuck in the recycling bin and he fell over onto his rump.

Ernie heard laughter from across the room. "I'm so sorry!" the voice said, still snickering.

As Ernie grew accustomed to the light, he saw a woman perched on a stool by the kitchen sink. From the laugh, Ernie recognized Cat Lady.

"Cat Lady!" he cried. "Gimme a heart attack!"

"I didn't mean to startle you," she said, still laughing. "And I hate to laugh. But I've never seen you dance before." She had been reading a newspaper in the fading light of the kitchen window. She fanned herself with it as she struggled to get her laughter under control.

48

"It's not that funny," muttered Ernie but then he added, "except I guess it is."

Cat Lady was the young woman who lived in the creepy cottage up the street with a gazillion cats in the yard. For several months, a persistent neighborhood rumor asserted that Cat Lady survived on fat cat stew. Ernie had already debunked that myth, but rumors have a way of hanging around. Many kids still thought Cat Lady was extremely weird, and maybe a bit crazy.

Dusty, for example, still hadn't made up his mind.

"She's not crazy," Ernie said, defending Cat Lady during recess.

"But all those cats!" cried Dusty.

"My dad says she's eccentric," Ernie said.

"What's 'eccentric'?" asked Dusty.

"It means 'unusual,'" Ernie explained.

"Unusual," Dusty repeated, singing through the word so that it sounded like a strange bird. "She's unusual all right."

Ernie knew there was more to Cat Lady than the "Cat Lady Legend" but it was still fun to tease her about all those cats. "Who's minding the cats, Cat Lady?" he said, crawling out of the recycling bin and kicking off his cleats.

"They're big enough to look after themselves," said Cat Lady.

"So am I," Ernie responded.

"Apparently not," Cat Lady replied. "Your dad called and asked me to watch you for the evening."

Ernie furrowed his brow. His brain was processing too much information. "Dad's not here?" he asked.

"He got offered a double shift at work. He won't be home until late," Cat Lady explained.

"So why'd he call you?" Ernie asked. He slugged his knapsack off his shoulders and threw it onto the floor.

Cat Lady leaned against the counter. "I told your dad to feel free to call on me if he ever needed backup in the kid department," she explained. She clasped her hands as though she had explained all she could.

"I'm not a baby," said Ernie.

"Take it up with your father," said Cat Lady, picking her battles wisely.

"Oh I will," said Ernie. "You can be sure of that."

"All I know is," Cat Lady continued, "Red got an extra shift at the plant and asked if I'd pitch in and watch the monster." She arched an eyebrow at Ernie and continued, "I'm guessing he was referring to you."

Ernie smirked. Cat Lady could be pretty funny at times. "What kind of monster?" he asked.

"The kind that clomps dirt into the house and throws stuff all over the floor," Cat Lady answered. "The very worst kind." Cat Lady waved a dish towel like it was the flag of peace. "Truce, truce," she cried.

Ernie laughed. He didn't really mind spending the evening with Cat Lady. It wasn't her fault she was stuck with this job. "Truce," he said and Cat Lady sighed demonstratively with relief.

Ernie grabbed an apple off the counter and bit into it. "So how'd you get inside?" he asked.

Cat Lady nudged around Ernie to reach the refrigerator door. "Your father told me about the key under the rock," she said.

Ernie tilted his head in surprise. The key under the rock was strictly confidential information. His father had given him strict instructions to never tell anyone about the key under the rock. "Dad told you about the key?" asked Ernie, like Cat Lady was suddenly a security risk.

"Everybody's got a key under the rock. That old trick," said Cat Lady with a sniff and a wave of her hand. She rattled the empty vegetable bins and screwed up her face like she was getting nowhere with this refrigerator. "Now, me personally," she continued, "I don't use a rock. I keep my key under one of the cats in the yard but you'll have to torture me before I tell you which one."

Ernie eyed Cat Lady. Sometimes, it was hard to tell whether she was being serious or not.

Cat Lady hadn't found anything of interest in the refrigerator. She yanked open the kitchen cupboards. They were loaded with cans. "Yowza," she said, eyeing the shelves, "you guys got enough cans to sink a battleship."

"Dad prefers the cans," said Ernie. "Every time we go shopping, he's always saying 'Be prepared, be prepared!'"

Cat Lady leaned back against the open cupboard doors. "We're just going to have to be creative," she said with a sly gleam. "Tell me, Ernie, what do you want for supper?"

"I'm a frozen pizza kid," he replied. "Just open the freezer. Nothing fancy. You want to hear our grocery list? Cans, toilet paper, pasta, cheese, ice cream sandwiches, and frozen pizza."

Cat Lady shuddered. "We can do better than that," she said. She jostled through cans on the shelf, uttering little grunts of approval until she had lined up four cans in a row on the counter. She turned toward Ernie, tapping her cheek with a finger, and asked pensively, "Now if I was a can opener, where would I be?"

Ernie started to answer but Cat Lady cut him off. "Wait, wait, don't tell me," she said. It was a test. She gazed from one end of the kitchen to the other and then tugged on the second drawer from the sink. She reached inside, found the can opener and shook it at Ernie. "Ta-da!" she cried triumphantly. "Can opener!"

"Lucky guess," said Ernie.

Cat Lady rattled the can opener like a saber and attacked one of the cans.

"What you got in mind with those cans?" asked Ernie.

"A surprise," Cat Lady answered, jerking her head toward the sink as if Ernie knew what to do with his hands.

"What kind of surprise?" Ernie persisted.

"Maybe a tuna surprise," said Cat Lady, holding the can by her face like a television spokesmodel. "I make a wonderful tuna surprise."

"What's so wonderful about it?" Ernie muttered. He tugged on the faucet and reached for the soap.

"Well, that's the surprise," Cat Lady said with a twinkle in her eye as she went from can to can with the can opener. "When something is wonderful, it's full of things you don't expect. Things you wonder about but don't want to ruin the surprise by asking what. You just have to trust it's good and go with the experience." Just like that, all four cans were opened.

"You're pretty good with that can opener," Ernie observed. He tossed the soap back into the dish and scrubbed his hands over the sink.

"Yes, well, that's what comes from living with cats,"

said Cat Lady. She checked the oven and let the door slam shut with a bang.

After dinner, Ernie patted his belly and let out a proud belch. "Wonderful," he cried. "Wonderful, wonderful, wonderful!"

"I'll take that as a compliment," said Cat Lady, glancing at Ernie's clean plate. "I gather you liked my Tuna Surprise," she said.

"Couldn't have been better," said Ernie. "I should have known you'd be good with a can of tuna." He grazed a hand over his nose and mewed like a kitten, "Meow!"

"Just wait till you taste what I can do with kidney and liver," Cat Lady said as she scooped up the plates to clear the table.

Ernie stood and stretched and let his uniform billow in all directions. The pants stretched thisaway and the shirt stretched thataway.

"I must say, Ernie," Cat Lady observed, "I didn't take you for the baseball type."

"I'm not," said Ernie. "I hate it."

Cat Lady dropped the dishes in the sink. "So why do you play?" she asked.

"I don't play," said Ernie. "I'm team manager."

"Ah!" said Cat Lady. "Well, that makes sense." She knew what Ernie could do with a business. "Although," she ventured further, as she studied Ernie's uniform, "would you allow me to do you a favor?"

"What's that, Cat Lady?"

"Let me take in that uniform for you," she said. "It's

way too big. You look like you're drowning."

"I knew it!" Ernie exclaimed. He stormed around the table, flinging his arms in exasperation. The sleeves billowed and bustled about him. "I look like ridiculous, don't I? I look like a clown!"

Cat Lady smiled. It was true. He did look like a clown. "The uniform could certainly use a little downsizing," she said. She tugged the loose fabric in Ernie's shirt and pinched a good two inches. "And aren't you lucky that I know how to use a needle and thread?"

"Knock yourself out," said Ernie.

Cat Lady gazed about the kitchen. "Now if I was a needle and thread," she said and let her voice trail off.

Ernie crossed his arms smugly. Cat Lady had just issued herself a challenge. "Maybe that's for me to know and for you to find out," he said.

Cat Lady crossed to the drawer directly beneath the telephone. She gave it a tug and looked inside. "Bingo," she cried. "The junk drawer!"

She pulled out a pin cushion containing several pins and both needle and thread. Ernie applauded and Cat Lady bowed. "Now stand on the chair," she said.

"Careful," Ernie advised, "my socks are kind of stinky."

"Too late," said Cat Lady. "I already noticed."

Ernie stood on the chair and Cat Lady set to work, pinning the fabric where she could make improvements.

"I owe you for this, Cat Lady," said Ernie.

"You don't owe me nothing," Cat Lady answered, with her mouth full of pins. She cleared her mouth so that she could be understood. "It's the least I can do for the Team

Manager of the Central Comets. Does this mean you're finally going to fix up that dump of a ballpark?"

Ernie bristled. "It is not such a dump!"

"It's a dump," said Cat Lady. "But if anybody could fix that place up, I'd put my money on you and Dusty."

Ernie bristled again. He didn't want to think about fixing that old dump of a ballpark. And he hadn't really thought about Dusty much at all.

"I can't wait to see what Dusty does with the place," said Cat Lady. "How is Dusty? I haven't seen him in a while."

"I think he's going through something," Ernie remarked, remembering what Swimming Pool had said. "He hasn't been around so much."

"Has he grown?" Cat Lady asked.

Ernie tried to think. It had been a while since he'd taken a good look at Dusty. "I guess," he said.

Cat Lady made one final adjustment to the uniform and whacked the back of the chair. "Okay, off," she said. "Time for your bath. And you're going to have to handle that on your own."

"Can do, Cat Lady," said Ernie. He hopped off the chair and began licking at his sleeves just like a cat.

Cat Lady threw a dish towel at Ernie. "Shoo, you!" she said. "Get into that tub! Oh, and toss that uniform downstairs so I can start stitching."

"Yes, ma'am!" Ernie cried, with another loud "Meow!" Ernie charged upstairs, still mewing as he scrambled on all fours.

Cat Lady pulled the needle from the pincushion and realized she didn't have nearly enough thread for the task at hand. She returned to the junk drawer and sorted through odds and ends until she found a spool of white thread. As she picked it up, she happened to notice a small yellow note underneath. She lifted the note into the light and read a message printed in blue ink in a woman's handwriting. "Eat your peas," it read.

Cat Lady flipped the note over but there was nothing on the other side. She dropped the note where she found it and closed the drawer with a bump of her hip.

"Cat Lady!" Ernie called from above.

She stepped into the hallway. "Yes," she answered, "you rang?"

Ernie leaned over the banister. "Hey, Cat Lady, did I say thank you? Thanks for watching me and thanks for the shirt and the pants and thanks for the wonderful tuna surprise."

Cat Lady smiled. She was about to say, "You're welcome" when Ernie's uniform landed on her head.

CHAPTER SEVEN

Life of the Party

Swimming Pool didn't know about the white gloves.

All she knew about charm school was that it happened at Miss Ginger's School of Tap & Tumbling. And she knew how to get to Miss Ginger's School of Tap & Tumbling because she had taken two years of gymnastics. She expected her mother to drop her off, as she always had, on the corner outside the mini-mall past the dry cleaners right next door to the school. Instead, her mother pulled into the parking lot and right up to the front door. Swimming Pool raised her eyebrows at the fancy treatment and reached for the car door. "So long, Mom!" she cried.

"Not so fast, buster," her mother said. She put the car into Park and turned toward Swimming Pool.

"What'd I do?" Swimming Pool asked suspiciously.

"Swimming Pool, I don't want a fight," her mother said as she reached under the seat to withdraw a slim blue shopping bag. She placed the bag on Swimming Pool's lap. "You're going to need these," she said. "Open and see."

Swimming Pool reached inside and pulled out two white cotton gloves. She dangled them for a better look. "Kind of dainty, don't you think?" she said, crinkling her nose.

"They're elegant," her mother said, reaching to pull off the sales tag.

"They're girlie," Swimming Pool groused.

"Now, Swimming Pool," her mother said, "I don't want a scene. Miss Ginger is very strict. Miss Ginger requires gloves. All the other girls will be wearing gloves."

"What for?" Swimming Pool asked, honestly curious, as she held the gloves in her extended fingers like a smelly wet rag.

"I don't know," her mother replied. "But it's tradition."

Swimming Pool could have asked a gazillion more questions but she was too nervous about charm school to put up a fight. "Whatever," she said. "No sweat, Mom. I can handle the gloves." She flung the gloves upward and caught them in her fist.

Her mother seemed surprised. "Really?" She had expected more of a fight.

"Sure," said Swimming Pool. "I wear a glove to baseball. I can wear a couple gloves for charm school. No big deal." Swimming Pool leaned over to give her mom a peck, stuffed the gloves in her own mouth and crawled out of the car.

"Swimming Pool," her mother admonished, "take those gloves out of your mouth."

Swimming Pool used both hands to slam the car door, took the gloves out of her mouth and leaned in through the window. "It takes both hands to close the door, Mom," she said. "I didn't want to dirty them up."

She ran to the front door of Miss Ginger's School of Tap & Tumbling and tugged one of the gloves onto her hand so she could turn around and wave good-bye to her mother just like a First Lady.

Swimming Pool's mother was so relieved about the white gloves that she didn't even notice that Swimming Pool was running into charm school wearing her favorite ripped-up red high-top sneakers.

Inside Miss Ginger's School of Tap & Tumbling, Swimming Pool felt a rush of memory at the sights and smells of the tumbling studio. Not so long ago, she had learned her cartwheels and handstands in this very room. Swimming Pool sighed at the memory of a near-perfect back flip, but then she remembered how hard she had jammed her big toe. It had hurt so bad that Swimming Pool still winced and said "Ouch!"

Of course, the tumbling studio had been completely transformed for charm school. A thin white drape covered the wall-sized mirrors. The tumbling mats had been stowed away. Card tables and folding chairs had been positioned across the floor. Each table was covered with a light blue cloth and held a small vase of fake flowers, pink and yellow, and four place settings consisting of a single cloth napkin.

Swimming Pool was impressed. Back in her tumbling days, they had been grateful for a few mats and a towel. "Miss

Ginger really went all out," she thought. "This place is the works!"

Swimming Pool was still marveling at the splendor of charm school when Miss Ginger appeared from the equipment closet at the far end of the hall. "Hi, Miss Ginger," Swimming Pool said brightly.

"Hello, little girl," Miss Ginger replied. She was toting a portable boom box and looking for a plug.

Swimming Pool flinched slightly. She didn't like being called a "little girl." She hadn't been a little girl for two years. She posed in the doorway in her new dress. "Don't you remember me?" she asked.

"Oh dear," said Miss Ginger, squatting in the corner to reach for an outlet, "there have been so many little girls."

"It's 'Swimming Pool,'" Swimming Pool replied, somewhat miffed. "Remember 'Swimming Pool'? I took tumbling from you for two years."

"Oh, yes, 'Swimming Pool'!" Miss Ginger replied, trying to mask her faulty memory with lots of enthusiasm. She plugged the boom box into the wall and rose to her feet, groaning slightly at the pain in her joints. Swimming Pool watched as Miss Ginger crossed the studio in long purposeful strides with her palm extended. She shook Swimming Pool's hand briskly and tilted her head to one side as she said, "Welcome back to Miss Ginger's!"

Swimming Pool was so bowled over that she completely forgot Miss Ginger's slight stumble over her name. Miss Ginger was the most glamorous woman she had ever met. Back in tumbling class, Miss Ginger always wore sweatsuit ensembles in solid air-freshener colors like pink, lavender, and a soft spearmint green. Today, Miss Ginger was all dolled up in a pretty dress with earrings and high-heeled shoes. Miss Ginger always seemed as cool as a convenience store on a hot summer day—and she smelled especially nice for charm school. It was the smell of new soap, fresh flowers, and a faint trace of nail polish remover. "I don't know how she does it," Swimming Pool thought.

"You'll excuse me, won't you, little girl?" Miss Ginger said, suddenly preoccupied. She pulled back the white drape, glanced at the mirror to check her teeth for lipstick, and smiled brightly at Swimming Pool. "There's so much to do before all the other little girls arrive!" With that said, Miss Ginger was gone.

"Oh, sure," said Swimming Pool. "Don't worry about me." But Miss Ginger had already swept into the outer office.

Swimming Pool was surprised to find that she was standing alone at charm school. "I must be early," she realized. Swimming Pool pulled back the white drape and blinked her eyes in the mirror. "I bet this is the first time I have ever been early in my life!" she thought. Swimming Pool quickly shook off the thought. It was mildly overwhelming. The dress and gloves were enough for one day. She didn't want to grow up so fast.

Fortunately, Swimming Pool wasn't alone for long. She was relieved to hear a voice say, "Swimming Pool, what are you doing here?" When she looked up, she saw Gina standing in the doorway.

Gina was the class brainiac at Swimming Pool's school. What Swimming Pool liked about Gina was that, smart as she was, she was also certifiably shy. "Swimming Pool!" Gina repeated, "I'm so glad to see somebody I know but of all people, I never expected you! Swimming Pool in charm school? Who'd a-thunk?" Swimming Pool was sure that Gina meant it in the nicest possible way.

"Charm school, busted," she replied. "But at least I got company. Your mom sign you up too?"

Gina nodded. "My mom says charm school is important for my permanent record," she said. Gina never did anything that wasn't good for her permanent record.

"So riddle me this, Gina," Swimming Pool said, holding out her gloves like a prizefighter. "Why the gloves?"

"I was going to ask you the same thing!" Gina replied, marveling at the coincidence.

Before they could unravel the mystery, they were interrupted by a bevy of girls in party dresses. They filed into the room, chattering nervously, and sure enough, they were all wearing gloves.

"Somebody's going to know about the gloves," said Swimming Pool, as they eyed the swelling ranks of their charm school class.

"Odds are," Gina agreed.

"Okay, I give," Swimming Pool observed. "Where are all the boys?"

"Boys?" Gina scoffed. "Boys never come to charm school!"

"How fair is that?" asked Swimming Pool.

"It's not," said Gina. "But somehow they get out of it."

The chatter of girls in the studio was getting to be really loud when Swimming Pool heard a small scream. Another voice cried, "Swimming Pool!" The room was getting crowded and it was hard to tell where the voice came from. "Over here, Swimming Pool! Come sit with us!"

Swimming Pool tracked down the voice and cringed slightly when she spotted Betty, an extremely domineering girl she'd known since kindergarten. Swimming Pool and Betty had been thrown together on several arranged play-dates over the years but it had never really worked out. "Oh, hi Betty," Swimming Pool said, without a lot of enthusiasm.

"Sit with us, sit with us!" Betty chimed, waving Swimming Pool over to her table. Betty was sitting with Kirsten, who was sort of Betty's first lieutenant.

"Hey, Kirsten," said Swimming Pool.

"Hey, Pool, I like your dress!" Kirsten gushed. "Isn't this exciting?" Kirsten was so excited about charm school that she couldn't stop fidgeting. The other two chairs at the table were occupied by Finny and Fanny, a rather eccentric set of identical twins with a fondness for bugs, secrets, and matching cardigan sweaters. Swimming Pool never felt entirely comfortable around Finny and Fanny.

"Sit with us, sit with us," chimed Betty, suddenly the life of the party. "I want Swimming Pool to sit with us!"

Swimming Pool hedged. "Aw, gee, I'd love to," she said, "but there are only four seats." Betty leaned across the table and laid down the law for Finny and Fanny. "Okay Finny, okay Fanny," she said, "one of you has got to go."

Finny and Fanny exchanged a look of resignation and launched into a round of rock-paper-scissors. Clearly they had been in this predicament before. When rock beat scissors, Fanny rose from her chair and scooched sideways to join a girl with braids and braces sitting by herself at the next table.

"But I was planning to sit with Gina," Swimming Pool protested. She gestured toward Gina who tagged along shyly behind her. "Stay, Fanny, stay," she continued. "We'll find seats somewhere else."

Betty growled with exasperation. It sounded like the foghorn of a ship that had decided not to come into harbor. "Always have to complicate things, don't you, Swimming Pool?" she huffed. She leaned across the table toward Finny and jerked a thumb at the next table. "Okay Finny," she said, "you're out of here too."

Finny rose to join Fanny. The two sisters exchanged a look. Their fate had been sealed.

"Have a seat!" Betty said, gesturing toward the now empty chairs. Betty and Kirsten giggled with excitement as Swimming Pool and Gina settled into their seats. Betty launched into a story about the grueling experience she'd had getting ready for charm school. "It took me two hours!" Betty groaned, twisting a flip in her hair and adjusting the puff in her sleeves.

Swimming Pool was relieved when Gina changed the subject. "Swimming Pool," said Gina, "I think I figured out why we have the gloves."

"Why is that, Gina?" Swimming Pool asked.

Gina gripped her palms together and eyed the room. "Germs," she said with an air of suspicion. "They're everywhere." She used one gloved finger to point here and there across the room. "Look in a microscope sometime. It's disgusting."

The din of conversation abruptly halted when Miss Ginger descended onto the room.

"We better be quiet now," said Swimming Pool to Gina, "charm school is about to begin."

CHAPTER EIGHT

Excuse Me

Miss Ginger breezed among the tables, tossing little winks and waves at the girls like she was distributing free perfume samples at the mall. "My name is Miss Ginger," she announced, "as if you didn't know!"

The girls giggled gamely. Betty and Kirsten shot up straight in their chairs, suddenly called to attention. There was a mild smattering of gloved applause for Miss Ginger but she deflected it.

"First things first," she continued, getting right down to business. "I need to say a few words about punctuality."

Betty flinched. Miss Ginger had stopped directly behind Swimming Pool. "If you are on time or even slightly early, there is no problem," Miss Ginger said, brushing her hand across Swimming Pool's shoulder as if to acknowledge a good example. Swimming Pool dropped her head and blushed. Betty's jaw dropped. Truthfully, all the girls were amazed at the irony that Swimming Pool was getting praise for being on time. It was pretty much a historical first.

Miss Ginger leveled her gaze on Betty and Kirsten. She seemed to target her next remarks directly at them and tersely enunciated every word. "If, on the other hand, you are late, even a mere ten minutes late, for whatever reason," she said, "you must approach your hostess with an apology and then seamlessly blend with the guests at the party." She sang the word "seamlessly" and glided across the floor as she did as if to demonstrate what she expected from the girls.

"I don't get it," Kirsten said to Betty. "Were we late?" Betty made a slashing motion across her lip like Kirsten should zip it.

"Whatever your excuse," Miss Ginger continued, glancing once again at Kirsten and Betty, "it is the guest's responsibility to make the problem disappear." She waved her hands in front of her face as if to eliminate all distress. "Whoosh, whoosh, whoosh!" she cried with her hands in motion. "Whoosh!"

None of the girls could resist practicing the "Whoosh" gesture with their own gloved hands. Swimming Pool moved her lips wordlessly with Miss Ginger. "Whoosh, whoosh, whoosh," she seemed to say, although she looked more like she was imitating a goldfish.

Miss Ginger clapped her hands to restore order. "And now," she trilled, "before we go any further, I have a big treat in store." The girls wiggled in giddy anticipation.

Miss Ginger flung her arms about the room and cried,

"Introductions!" The girls looked at each other blankly but no one said a word. Miss Ginger flung her hands over the tables like she was shooing pigeons. "Go on! Go ahead!" she cried. "Introduce yourselves! It's easy!"

Swimming Pool exchanged glances with Betty, Kirsten, and Gina. These girls had known each other all their lives. Swimming Pool and Betty went back to preschool. Introductions hardly seemed necessary. Even so, the girls obediently raised gloved hands to wave at each other.

Swimming Pool flapped both hands like she was waving into a television camera. "Hey, Gina. Hey, Kirsten. Hey, Betty," she said. She twisted in her chair to wave at the next table. "Hey, Finny. Hey, Fanny. Hey, girl-I-don't-know-with-the-braces-and-braids." Finny and Fanny waved back. The girl with the braces and braids smiled.

Miss Ginger flickered the light switch in the studio to get everyone's attention. Many girls groaned slightly because the flickering lights were really annoying. When the room came to order, Miss Ginger continued. But the girls immediately noticed that Miss Ginger's attitude had changed.

Instead of the hospitable hostess, Miss Ginger had taken on the stern demeanor of a drill sergeant. "In the next few weeks, we're going to tackle some pretty challenging stuff! Be prepared for really tough words like 'curtsy,' 'comportment,' and 'etiquette'!" Miss Ginger scrutinized the room as though the girls should already know what she was talking about, though many of them didn't. "And perhaps the toughest word of them all," she added with an air of suspense. "Charm!"

Many girls inched a little taller in their seats as if they

had finally graduated to princess-in-training and were being outfitted for tiaras.

"How many of you girls know what I mean when I say the word 'charm'?" Miss Ginger asked, magnanimously. "Let's see a show of hands!" A few girls were tempted to raise their hands at Miss Ginger's direction but the wiser girls at each table recognized the shell game and stopped them with a look. Miss Ginger nodded slightly. She had expected as much. "Well, then," she said in a tone that meant business, "we've got a lot of work to do."

And then, quite unexpectedly, Miss Ginger brightened altogether. It was as if to demonstrate that a changeable mood was something girls could practice themselves once they understood "charm" more fully. "But for today," Miss Ginger continued, spreading her arms with a big smile, "the hard work can wait! Because today we are simply going to get acquainted!"

She laughed merrily and swept among the tables, throwing lots of sashay into her walk to make her energy infectious. "Let's fill this room with chatter!" she said. "Go ahead! Talk among yourselves! And in the meantime, I'll be serving punch and cookies!"

Kirsten leaned across the table and hissed at Swimming Pool. "Swimming Pool, Swimming Pool!"

"You don't have to whisper," Betty sneered.

Kirsten retreated slightly. "I just want to know how long this lasts," she said.

"I think we got another hour," Swimming Pool said. The table groaned.

"Punch time!" Miss Ginger cried as she reached Swimming Pool's table with a tray covered with cups. "It's lemonade spritzer!" she gushed. Each girl took a cup from the tray.

"What's in it?" Kirsten asked, examining her cup and wrinkling her nose.

Miss Ginger lowered her voice like she was sharing a secret recipe. "It's ordinary lemonade, no mystery there," she said, "mixed with sparkling water for a little kick. That's what gives it the 'punch'!" With that, Miss Ginger moved to the next table.

"Who wants mine?" said Swimming Pool. There were no takers. She shrugged with resignation and took a sip. The girls leaned in to gauge her reaction. Swimming Pool smacked her lips sharply. "Watered-down lemonade," she announced, "and pretty disgusting."

"Pretty ick," said Betty, after a tentative sip of her own. She shoved her cup to the center of the table.

"I bet it's not even real lemonade," said Gina. "I bet it's loaded with chemicals." Gina held her cup in both hands and, as the girls watched in amazement, she tilted her head and knocked back her punch like a mad scientist with a potion. Gina put down the cup and smiled politely. Then the girls continued to watch as Gina went one amazing step further.

Gina burped.

It was a loud, deep, rich burp. Betty and Kirsten were dumbstruck. "Excuse me," Gina said, smiling shyly.

Swimming Pool applauded with her gloved hands.

"Whoa, good one," she cried. "You should come to my house, Gina. I've got six brothers who have a burping contest at the dining room table. You'd be the new champ!"

"A burping contest?" asked Kirsten. "What's that?"

"Some rude boy thing," said Swimming Pool. "The winner is the one who burps the loudest but they've got all sorts of crazy categories for most congenial and most creative. Stuff like that."

"What's 'most congenial' about a burp?" asked Betty.

"My brother Eddie burped 'Hello' into the answering machine," Swimming Pool explained.

"And what was 'most creative'?" asked Kirsten.

"My brother Danny," said Swimming Pool. "He can belch and sing at the same time."

Kirsten and Gina murmured "Whoa" in admiration. "Oh, he cannot!" said Betty dismissively.

"Come to my house if you don't believe me," said Swimming Pool. "I've heard him burp his way through the 'Star-Spangled Banner.'"

"How does he do that?" asked Gina, already examining the implications of such a thing.

"I want to go!" cried Kirsten. "I want to hear!" She raised her gloved hand as if to say, "Choose me!" Betty threw Kirsten a look and Kirsten slowly lowered her hand.

"It sounds disgusting!" said Betty. "Why do boys have to belch like that? I think burping is vulgar!"

"Oh, me, too," said Swimming Pool. She took a deep gulp of air, turned in Betty's direction and delivered a loud burp. Gina and Kirsten laughed.

"It's a contest!" cried Kirsten, reaching for her cup. "Let's have our own contest!"

"Oh, I don't know," said Swimming Pool, casting a nervous glance around the room. "That might upset Miss Ginger."

Kirsten had already slurped her lemonade spritzer. She gulped deeply and croaked, "I don't care!" The words were gift-wrapped in a resounding belch. Naturally, the girls burst into giggles. Gina grabbed Betty's leftover cup and cried, "My turn!" Before long, the girls were working on their personal best and issuing challenge-burps. Even Finny, Fanny, and the girl with the braids and braces joined the fray.

The only girl not competing was Betty. She glowered miserably as though she was sitting among barbarians.

Swimming Pool couldn't resist the fun. She took another swig of punch, gulped some air, and warmed up her boardinghouse special.

Unfortunately, at that same moment, Miss Ginger descended on the table, flapping her hands so fast they almost fell off. "Whoosh, whoosh, whoosh!" she cried. "Whoosh, whoosh!"

Swimming Pool truly meant to say, "Excuse me, Miss Ginger!" but the words came out snuggling under a burp overcoat. Miss Ginger looked aghast. All the girls laughed and chimed in.

"Excuse me, Miss Ginger! Excuse me!" they croaked. The table had turned from a lovely circle of girls in party dresses into a pack of merry frogs perched on a lily pad.

Betty shoved back in her chair. "I had nothing to do with this, Miss Ginger," she declared. "The belching contest was Swimming Pool's idea!"

"It was not," Swimming Pool protested.

"You brought it up!" Betty argued.

"It's not my fault," cried Swimming Pool. "It's the lemonade spritzer!"

Miss Ginger was smiling but she didn't seem very happy. "Swimming Pool, could I have a word with you for a moment, please?"

Miss Ginger pulled Swimming Pool out of her chair and close to the white drape. She leaned in close without letting go of Swimming Pool's arm. "Perhaps I neglected to mention the number-one rule of Charm School," Miss Ginger said, in a tone that was not very nice at all. "Three strikes and you're out!" She held up one gloved finger in Swimming Pool's face and announced, "Strike number one."

CHAPTER NINE

Last One Left

It was Dusty's turn to be miserable.

Another wild pitch whizzed past his head. The bullpen went "crash-bang" as the ball slammed into the chain-link fence. "Sorry!" cried Larry, the designated relief pitcher. Dusty's arms were still wrapped over his head. He felt like a sitting duck.

Dusty unwrapped himself and scrambled to retrieve the ball in the dirt. It was bad enough that just as Dusty had gotten the hang of catching the ball, Swimming Pool had bailed to go to charm school. With Swimming Pool gone, Dusty figured he'd be able to hang out with Ernie but Ernie had become all buddy-buddy with Kip, the captain. Dusty felt like he was all by himself on a team full of Comets. It was like he was the last one left.

To make matters worse, not only was he a sitting duck, but he had to throw the ball back to Larry on the pitcher's mound for another chance at beaning his head. Dusty threw the ball to Larry as hard as he could. Larry backpedaled and twisted his mitt underhanded but he managed to catch the ball all the same. He held up the ball to show that it had arrived. "The next one will be better," Larry cried. "I promise!"

Dusty squatted behind the plate, adjusted his mask and cringed.

"Crash-bang." After the next wild pitch smashed into the bullpen, Dusty unwrapped himself and was about to retrieve the ball from the dirt. Before he could, he heard voices cry, "Dusty! Hey, Dusty! Come over here! Dusty!"

Dusty took off his mask and peered down the third base line. Ernie and Kip were gesturing wildly for him to join them.

"What do you want?" Dusty hollered.

"We gotta talk about something," cried Kip.

Dusty signaled "take five" to Larry on the pitcher's mound. It was a slash at the throat and a spread of five fingers. Larry seemed to understand.

Dusty ditched his catcher's mask at home plate and trotted down the third base line for the official word with Ernie and Kip.

"Before you get started," said Dusty as he arrived, "it's not because I'm afraid of the ball."

"It's not about the ball," said Ernie.

"We see you been good with the ball," Kip agreed with a chuckle. "That Larry is a wild man."

"We got a special job for you, Dusty," said Ernie. "Boy,

are you gonna be happy." Dusty thought that Ernie was smiling a bit too wide. In fact, Kip was also smiling too wide. The two boys were showing so many teeth that Dusty felt like he was negotiating with crocodiles.

"A special job doing wha-aat?" Dusty responded, more than a little suspicious.

"You know how we're always complaining about what a dump the ballpark is?" Ernie began. Ernie had an elaborate plan for luring Dusty into their ballpark renovation proposal but his plan never got off the launch pad. Before Ernie could finish his first sentence, Kip blurted out, "Yeah, right. Look, Dusty, we want you to paint the ballpark."

Ernie threw Kip a look as if to say, "Let me handle this," but it was too late. "Paint the ballpark!" Dusty cried, heading for a tantrum.

"Dusty, Dusty, Dusty," Ernie said, trying to calm the waters. He started over from the top. "You know how we're always complaining about what a dump the ballpark is?"

"I don't think it's a dump," said Dusty. "I think the ballpark is charming!"

"Well, we think it needs to be spruced up a bit," said Kip.

"Spruced up?" Dusty asked, not believing his ears. "So—you want me to scrape the gum off the bleachers, pick up the hotdog wrappers, and empty the garbage?" Dusty was quickly picking up steam.

"No, no, no," said Ernie. "Dusty, Dusty, Dusty. We were thinking more about the artistic side of things."

Dusty was ready for another outburst but he paused slightly to cock his head and repeat, "The artistic side?" Art was always music to his ears.

Before Ernie could continue, Kip dove in again. "Yeah, artistic, like paint the back wall," he said. He pointed to the broken-down wooden wall that surrounded the entire outfield. "We heard you got lots of paint and stuff."

Dusty exploded. "Paint the back wall?" he cried. Dusty launched into a lengthy tirade about the impropriety of squandering an artistic nature on a rudimentary project like "painting the back wall." It went on for close to a minute. Eventually, Kip ducked behind Ernie for cover.

Ernie took his time to do a casual about-face, slowly revolving like a classroom globe. When he reached Kip, he crossed his eyes and wrenched his mouth as if to say Kip should put a sock in it or Ernie was going to scream. When Ernie rotated back to Dusty, his face was back to its usual, sweet, smiling self.

"Dusty, Dusty, Dusty," Ernie said, his voice full of appreciation, "you know you're the only man for this job! We need someone with your special talents and your particular gifts. Who else could we ask?"

Dusty wasn't sure he was supposed to answer that question but, in truth, nobody else came to mind.

Ernie wrapped an arm around Dusty's shoulders. "We want someone who can give this ballpark a complete makeover," he said.

Dusty was inclined to argue, but he found himself stumbling over what Ernie had said. "Did you say 'a complete makeover'?" he asked.

"And you're the only man for the job," Ernie repeated, savoring the moment. He felt sure that he had hooked Dusty. It was like he had Dusty in the palm of his hand.

Unfortunately, Kip chose that moment to blurt out, "Yeah, come on, Dusty. Do it for the team."

Dusty balked all over again. "'Do it for the team'?" he cried. "How stupid do you think I am? Do I look like I just fell off a swing?"

Ernie drew Dusty farther down the third base line. "Walk with me, Dusty," he said. "Walk with me." He threw Kip a look that said, "Thanks a lot! Damage control."

Kip spanked his hands clean of the problem and kept his distance.

When Ernie and Dusty had stepped out of Kip's earshot, Dusty muttered, "Sometimes you take the cake, Ernie, you really do."

"What'd I do?" said Ernie. "What's going on, Dusty? What is it with you? I thought you'd be flattered."

"Paint the wall?" Dusty repeated. "Look at the size of that thing!"

"Admit it," said Ernie. "If we had asked anybody else, you'd be insulted."

"I'm insulted already," said Dusty. "I don't appreciate the hot-box. If you wanted to ask me for a favor, you could have asked me yourself."

"It's not a favor for me," said Ernie. "It's for the whole team. And besides, Kip is the captain."

"I know Kip is the captain," said Dusty. "You don't have to explain to me how Kip is the captain." Dusty got quiet for a moment. He didn't want to talk about it.

"And so what?" Ernie asked impatiently. "What is it with you, Dusty?"

Dusty kept his voice low and didn't look Ernie in the

eyes. "Where you been, Ernie?" he said. "We used to be friends. I joined the Comets to be near you and Swimming Pool. But now Swimming Pool is gone."

"She'll be back," said Ernie. "We're only losing her to charm school for a few practice sessions. She'll be back for the games."

"I know she'll be back," said Dusty. "But she's not here. And you don't have time for me. You got your fancy new team-captain friend. I feel all alone. Do you know how that feels? I feel like the last one left."

There was nothing Ernie could say. Ernie and Dusty used to be inseparable but lately he hadn't been hanging with Dusty like the old days.

"Okay, fine," said Ernie. "Don't paint the wall."

"I'll paint it," said Dusty. "I don't care. It's not about the wall."

"No," said Ernie. "I don't want you painting the wall. I'll get somebody else."

"I said I'll paint the wall," Dusty asserted, like there was no letting go. "Just don't make a big deal about it."

Ernie held his hands up. "O-kay," he said. "Have it your way."

They headed down the base line to the spot where Kip was waiting, seated in the grass. "It's fixed," Ernie said as Kip stood up and brushed off his pants. "He'll do it."

"Excellent," said Kip, nodding at Dusty. He pulled off his cap and mopped his brow. "Listen, I been thinking," he continued. "The back wall is a big job for one kid. Maybe we should get the team to help."

"I don't need any help," Dusty protested.

"Kip's right," said Ernie. "Think about it, Dusty. We can get you a crew. You're going to need helpers."

"So it's settled," said Kip. "We're gonna have a brand-new ballpark."

"Not quite," said Dusty. "I still don't have enough paint to do that whole wall."

"Don't worry about it," said Ernie. "I just figured out where we can find all the paint in the world."

Kip and Dusty looked at Ernie with surprise. "Where?" they asked.

Ernie stretched his arm to point across the field. "The Moose Lodge," he said, like that answered everything.

Kip and Dusty followed Ernie's arm to a building on the far side of the back wall, beyond where Ernie and Dusty had just been standing. It was a short, dilapidated building but the exterior had recently been covered in a fresh coat of paint. "Oh," said Dusty and Kip, taking the word on a roller-coaster to show they had caught on.

"Just follow the smell of fresh paint," said Ernie, "and we should find all we need."

Kip patted him on the back. "Good job, Ernie," he said.

"There's one thing I still don't understand," said Dusty, arching an eyebrow like he'd never heard anything so ridiculous. "What's a Moose Lodge?" he said.

CHAPTER TEN

The Moose Lodge

Ernie and Dusty headed for the Moose Lodge after practice. They weren't halfway across the outfield and Dusty was already brainstorming plans for the back wall.

"I could paint more people," Dusty enthused. "Like more bleachers, completely surrounding the park."

Ernie almost regretted suggesting Dusty in the first place. "Dusty," he sighed, "all we want is paint on a wall."

"But that's so boring!" said Dusty. "This could be my Mona Lisa, my Sistine Chapel, my Mount Rushmore, my—"

"Paint on a wall," Ernie repeated, like he was ordering a menu item and fighting with the waiter. "Paint. Just paint. All we asked for was paint."

The Moose Lodge sat on an empty parking lot. A wide stair-well and a handicap ramp led to the front porch. The building almost looked like somebody's private home except the front door was made of glass and you could see a fire extinguisher and a pay phone in the front hall.

Ernie rang the doorbell, but nobody answered.

"Doesn't look like the moose are at home," said Dusty.

"The parking lot is empty," Ernie observed. "But the parking lot is always empty."

"Maybe the moose moved away," said Dusty with a shrug.

Ernie tried the thumb-latch on the door handle and, to his surprise, the door swung wide open. Ernie and Dusty jumped back. "Uh-oh," said Dusty. "We're in trouble now."

Ernie shrugged. "Maybe it's always open," he said. "Maybe the Moose Lodge is like a business."

"I don't think so," said Dusty. "I have never heard of moose selling anything."

"They're not that kind of moose, Dusty." Ernie stepped across the threshold.

"Then what kind of moose are they?" Dusty asked as he followed behind.

The front hall smelled of musk and floor wax. It smelled like the windows and doors hadn't been opened in a long time. "This place needs a good airing out," said Ernie.

"Smells like my grandmother's attic," Dusty agreed.

"Hello!" said Ernie.

Nobody answered. "Nobody home," said Dusty. "Let's get out of here."

"Hold on," said Ernie. "Listen." He cupped a hand to his ear. A radio was playing somewhere deep inside the Moose Lodge. "Somebody's home," Ernie continued. "Let's check it out."

Dusty dragged his feet as they headed down the hall. "I don't know about this," he muttered. Dusty followed Ernie down the hallway with tentative steps. Ernie called "Hello" at every open door they passed, but all they heard was the echo of Ernie's own voice.

Dusty thought it was really creepy. The first room held file cabinets. The next room held supersized floral tributes but the flowers had long since wilted and died. Another room was full of teapots, plates, and big silver coffee urns. "This place is like a spook house," Dusty said with a shiver.

"That's what I was thinking," said Ernie. "Are you scared?" Truthfully, Ernie was a little spooked himself.

"'Course I'm scared," said Dusty. "When I build a spook house, I'm not scared—but this place is for real."

At the end of the hall was a wide stairwell. The music was louder upstairs. Ernie threw a look at Dusty as if to say, "No retreat and no surrender." He grabbed onto the railing and started to climb. Dusty followed but he held onto Ernie's shirttail for security.

Halfway up the stairwell, Ernie announced, "There's your moose!"

"Where?" asked Dusty, swiveling from side to side as though he had missed a ghost.

"Behind you," Ernie answered, "on the walls."

The walls of the stairwell were lined with large picture frames. Dusty took a closer look and saw that each frame contained a fancy scroll banner that read: "The Grand Order of Moose." Underneath the banner were several rows of small photographs. And each photograph seemed to be the head of another little old man with thick black eyeglasses and a funny mustache. It looked like the grandfathers' club had lined up for school photographs. Each face was identified but the old men had curious names—names so old they might as well have been dinosaurs.

"Check out the names," Dusty said with a laugh. "Mortimer, Sylvester, Clarence, and Otto!"

"I got Eunice and Magnolia over here," said Ernie. He was looking at framed photographs of women on the opposite wall. "It says the Daughters of the American Revolution but they all look like grandmothers to me."

"How old are these?" asked Dusty.

"Old," Ernie answered. "Probably wartime."

The radio was louder at the top of the stairs but it was accompanied by a mechanical hum so loud that the floor vibrated under their feet. Dusty grabbed Ernie's shirttail so tight that it tugged on his collar. "Ease up, Dusty," Ernie said. "You're choking me."

The stairwell opened onto a large banquet room. A fine wooden floor stretched from one end of the room to the other. It would have been perfect for a basketball game except for the large wagon-wheel chandelier that hung over the center of the room. Heavy curtains covered the windows. At the far end of the hall was a small stage, same as a school cafetorium.

The radio was even louder in the banquet room and

from this angle, Ernie and Dusty could see a boom box perched on the edge of the stage. The boom box was tuned to a station that played big band swing music. Golden oldies bounced off the walls.

In front of the stage, Ernie saw a small boy maneuvering a large floor waxer. It was a big, heavy machine with circular pads on the bottom that chugged and clattered across the floor. The boy was scrambling to keep up with the waxer, but he was jittering and jiggling so much that it almost looked like he was dancing. The boy turned one way, the waxer turned another, and the boy slid nimbly out of the way as the waxer took an elegant spin. It took Ernie only a moment to conclude that the boy was, in fact, dancing—and dancing with a machine.

"Don't I know that kid?" said Dusty.

"Of course you do," said Ernie. He held a hand to his mouth and called out above the music, "Tony! Hey, Tony!"

The kid on the waxer looked up with surprise. Boys don't like to be caught dancing. Sure enough, it was Tony.

Tony was known around the neighborhood for being short and industrious. Ernie had never seen Tony when he wasn't working somebody for a quarter, a dime, or even a nickel. For a long time, Tony had been in business with a shovel. "Hey, Tony!" Ernie called. "I'm surprised to see you without your shovel."

Tony jumped back, startled. He turned off the waxer as though he had only realized that the waxer had been on.

Ernie hadn't meant to startle Tony quite so badly. "It's Ernie," he cried. "Ernie Castellano. And I'm here with Dusty."

"Oh, hey, Ernie. Hey, Dusty," Tony said. He wrestled

with the waxer as if he'd been having a difficult time getting it to work right. "What are you guys doing here?"

"Snooping," said Dusty. "What are you doing here?"

"Me?" said Tony. "I work here." He threw the switch on the waxer and went back to work on the floor. Tony knew just how loud to talk to be heard over the machine. "Actually, my dad's the caretaker," he explained. "I just help out for spare change."

"You had me scared for a moment," said Ernie. "It looked like you were dancing with the waxer."

"Dancing with the waxer?" Tony snorted. The idea was ridiculous. "Right!"

"But he *was* dancing with the waxer," said Dusty. Ernie threw a quick elbow to encourage Dusty to be quiet.

"Well, this is quite a fortunate coincidence, Tony," said Ernie. "The Dust Man and I were hoping to run into you. We figured you might know where we could put our hands on some paint."

"Paint? What kind of paint?" asked Tony.

"House paint," said Dusty. "We got a big project on our hands."

"How big?" asked Tony.

"As big as the ballpark," said Dusty.

"That's big," Tony concluded.

"Any chance you got that kind of paint around here?" asked Ernie.

"I'll have to ask my dad," said Tony, "but I think we can work something out."

"Excellent," said Ernie.

"On one condition," Tony added.

"Name it," said Ernie.

Tony flipped off the waxer and leaned close to Ernie. He lowered his voice. The matter was strictly confidential. "Don't be mouthing off about me and the waxer," he said.

"Tony," Ernie answered in a sincere tone, "I'm surprised at you."

After Ernie and Dusty reclaimed their backpacks from the dugout, Dusty walked Ernie to the bike rack. "I'd say we got a lot accomplished in one afternoon," Ernie said as he unlocked his bicycle.

"I dunno," said Dusty, still eyeing the size of the ballpark. "We still got our work cut out for us." Dusty tore a page off a notepad in his hand and handed the message to Ernie. "What's this?" Ernie asked. "A bill?"

"It's a list of colors I'm interested in," said Dusty. "For when you meet with Tony and his dad about the Moose Lodge paint."

Ernie looked at the list. Dusty had written down enough colors to paint a full rainbow. "I don't know if he's gonna have this many colors, Dusty," he said.

"This is very important," Dusty urged. "If I can't get the colors on this list, it's going to upset all my plans for the ballpark."

Ernie eyed his backpack. "Tell you what," he said. "I'll stow the list in my backpack for safekeeping."

"Ouch," said Dusty. "You put it in that backpack and we'll never see it again. That backpack is a bottomless pit. Put it in the little zipper pocket that kids never use. That way it'll be safe."

Ernie rolled his eyes slightly. Dusty could be so demanding. Even so, Ernie said, "Good thinking!" and opened the zipper pocket to stow the message inside. As he slid his hand inside the pocket, however, Ernie found another piece of paper inside.

"What's this?" he asked. He pulled out his hand and revealed the second piece of paper. "Somebody slipped me a note," said Ernie.

"How do you know?" Dusty asked.

"I never use that pocket," said Ernie.

Dusty peered over his shoulder to look at the note. "So what's the note say?" asked Dusty.

Ernie unfolded the note. It had been written on a small yellow paper and folded several times. As Ernie unfolded it, glitter fell onto his hand. "It's a note in glitter," he said.

"Glitter?" asked Dusty. That didn't make sense.

"Look at my hand," said Ernie. He held out his hand and, sure enough, flecks of glitter were stuck to his fingertips.

Now Dusty was really curious. "So what's the note say, Ernie?" he asked. "Read it to me!"

Ernie glanced at the words and shut the note quickly. He tucked the note back into the zipper pocket and slung his knapsack back over his shoulder. "None of your beeswax," he said. "You walking home or you want to ride the handlebars?"

Dusty opted to climb onto the handlebars since it was a short ride. Ernie kept the conversation light during the ride so that Dusty wouldn't ask any more questions about the note.

Even so, Ernie couldn't take his mind off the note during the whole bike ride home. He hadn't wanted to share the message with Dusty because he hadn't really understood the message himself. But as he pedaled, Ernie couldn't forget the words.

The note in glitter read: "I know who likes you."

CHAPTER ELEVEN

Five O'Clock Shadow

Ernie charged through the front door, giving it just enough of a shove to shut tight and not so much that his dad would yell at him for slamming the door. He bolted upstairs, taking the steps two at a time. He grabbed onto the banister for the booster-push past the landing and up the last four steps.

If he hit the old Persian runner at the right angle, he could cruise down the hallway like he was riding a flying carpet. And in fact, Ernie was cruising neatly past the bathroom door when he heard an unlikely sound.

It was whistling.

Ernie called out, "Dad?" He heard the faucet squeak and water gush into the basin. He tapped at the door with his knuckle—but his tap couldn't compete with the happy little whistle, so finally Ernie banged on the door with his fist. "Dad!" he hollered.

It was the "Dad" that did it.

The door creaked open and released a gust of hot steam into the hall. Beyond the steam, he could see his father, perched over the sink. He was wrapped in his bathrobe with a handful of shaving cream.

"What do you want?" said Red.

"Home early?" asked Ernie.

"It's not that early," said Red.

"Oh," said Ernie. He meant to ask what Red was doing taking a shower but it seemed like a stupid question. "Hey, Dad," he continued, "I been meaning to ask you. Can you ask your sheet-metal boss to sponsor our team?"

Red patted his face with shaving cream until he had a Santa Claus beard. "Sponsor the team?" he said. "Didn't you already hit up the hardware store?"

"That was for uniforms," Ernie continued. "We need padded cushions for the bleacher seats. They're metal. It's uncomfortable. They heat up too much in the sun."

"Padded cushions?" Red asked, preoccupied with shaving cream. "Fancy."

"Those square things," Ernie explained. "It'll only be a couple hundred bucks. Tell them it's free advertising and it's for a good cause."

"I'll think about it," said Red.

"Don't just think about it," Ernie argued. "Show some initiative, Dad!"

"I said I'll think about it," Red repeated. He turned toward Ernie with a full face of lather. He looked kind of goofy.

"I'm glad I don't have to shave," said Ernie. He was ready to leave the bathroom when suddenly it occurred to him. It was almost dinnertime—and Red was shaving. Normally Red shaved in the morning. "Little late for a shave, isn't it, Dad?" he asked.

Red studied his face in the mirror. "I got five o'clock shadow," he said. "That's when you get scruffy in the middle of the afternoon and need to shave again."

Ernie leaned against the doorjamb. "But the day's over, Pop," he continued. "You can pack it in. Kick back. Watch TV. Fall asleep on the sofa."

"I'm going out tonight, Ernie," Red said.

"Ah-ha!" Ernie cried as though he had uncovered the mystery. Except, of course, that still didn't explain everything. "And who and what and where and when and why?" Ernie asked.

Red dragged another panel of shaving cream off his cheek. "I'm going out with a friend," he said.

"A friend?" said Ernie, enjoying the interrogation. "Do I know this friend? Have I met this friend?"

"Yes, I think you have," said Red. He navigated his jaw-line and appraised the results in the mirror, rubbing his chin thoughtfully like he was one of the three little pigs. "Ernie," he continued, enunciating carefully, "I got a date."

Red dropped the bomb and went back to shaving.

Ernie's jaw dropped open wide. "A date?" he repeated, even though he had heard Red loud and clear. "A date with a girlfriend? Is that what we're talking?"

"Well, she's a girl and she's a friend, but I wouldn't say a girlfriend."

"Dad," Ernie protested. "A girl and a date equals girlfriend. I wasn't born yesterday."

Red slapped his face with aftershave. "You're the one who said I should show some initiative," he said. "You're the one who said I should make new friends." He opened the medicine chest and grabbed a little sample bottle of cologne.

"Cologne? Cologne?" Ernie erupted incredulously. "Suddenly it's Prom Night?"

"Cologne is just something you wear to make a nice impression," said Red.

"Sure—and stink," said Ernie, pinching his nose.

Red replaced the bottle on the shelf and turned toward Ernie. "Look, Ernie, do you want me to cancel? Are you uncomfortable with this? Am I dating too soon? I miss your mother too, but if you think I need to give it more time—"

"Dad," Ernie interrupted, "I'm giving you a hard time. I'm poking fun. I want you to go on a date. To tell you the truth, it's kind of funny. You're so nervous and jumpy and everything."

"I guess I am nervous," Red admitted.

"Easy on the cologne, Dad," said Ernie. "So, is Cat Lady coming over?"

Red eyed him strangely. "How did you guess?"

"She's your last-minute cover, right? Like the time last week when you got an extra shift. Remember? Cat Lady came over."

Red nodded as if it had only just occurred to him. "Oh yeah, I remember," he said. "Cat Lady."

"Which is okay by me only as long as she comes here,"

Ernie said pointing at the floor of their house. "'Cause I'm not spending the night at her place with all those cats."

Red toweled off his face. "Actually," he said, "I didn't ask Cat Lady to watch you. I called one of Swimming Pool's brothers to come over."

Ernie balked. "Those jerks!" he protested. "All they do is play video games, pinch my ears, and burp and curse and fart on my bed!"

"Be-cause," Red continued, laying into the word with emphasis as though Ernie should shut up or he was going to miss the big news.

Ernie knew the code. "Because why?"

"Be-cause," Red said, taking his good sweet time to tug the last trace of shaving cream off his left ear, "the date is with Cat Lady."

At first Ernie didn't seem to hear the news. His serene expression didn't change at all. But it was only a moment before his brain had opened the mail and read the news.

That was when Ernie freaked. He threw himself against the doorjamb with both hands and feet. His face went wild-eyed and his hair stood on end. "Cat Lady?" Ernie cried with alarm.

"That's what I said," answered Red, nudging Ernie back into the hall. He chucked a bath towel with one hand and pressed the door closed with the other. "Cat Lady."

"But, Dad!" Ernie began to cry—and before the words could escape his mouth, the bath towel had hooked his head and draped him like a shroud. The bathroom door latched shut with a click. Ernie stood in the hall looking like a forgotten ghost in an empty, haunted house when it wasn't even

Halloween. And his scream was muffled by a wet bath towel.

"—not Cat Lady!"

Ernie stayed in his room for the next couple hours. He didn't even open the door when his dad knocked to say, "Okay, good-bye. I'm going now." Ernie was trying to get his thoughts together. This was no easy trick because Ernie's thoughts were zinging all over the place. One moment, they dodged easy answers; the next, they jumped to conclusions.

When Ernie finally crept downstairs, the house was empty except for the sound of the television. Ernie stepped into the den to find Brian, one of Swimming Pool's brothers, flopped on the sofa with the video game controls. He grunted as Ernie entered the room but, otherwise, he did not speak.

"My dad split?" Ernie asked.

"Don't talk to me," Brian barked, glued to the game. "Asteroid Attack! I'm up to level three!"

"Level three is for losers," Ernie said.

"I said don't talk to me," hollered Brian.

Ernie rolled his eyes and went back to his room. He parked himself at his desk and tried to do math homework but the numbers didn't make any sense. He sneaked into his dad's bedroom and turned on the smaller television set that allowed him to lose a couple hours on infomercials and game shows.

Eventually, Ernie heard his father's keys in the door. He turned off the television and scrambled down the hall as fast as he could. Listening from the upstairs landing, he heard Red enter the front hall. To his surprise, he also heard Cat

Lady's voice, laughing over some little something.

Ernie's jaw dropped, even though no one could see it. That little laugh could only mean one thing. Cat Lady was coming inside.

Ernie ducked out of sight and crawled from shadow to shadow down the upstairs hall. Moments later, listening down the back stairwell, Ernie heard Red talking with Brian, Swimming Pool's brother, in the kitchen.

"I think he went to bed early," Brian was saying.

"Early?" said Red. "That's not like Ernie."

Brian didn't seem concerned. "I asked him if he wanted to play 'Asteroid Attack,'" said Brian. "But he didn't seem interested. Do you know 'Asteroid Attack'? 'Cause I just made it all the way to level five."

Ernie scoffed from his upstairs perch. "Level five is for amateurs," he said to himself. He assumed that his dad paid Brian a few bucks because he heard Brian leave by the back door. He hugged the corner as he heard footsteps in the downstairs hallway. His dad said, "Ernie must have gone to sleep," and then Ernie couldn't hear any more. He assumed that Cat Lady and Red had gone into the living room.

Ernie didn't think he was actually eavesdropping because, after all, this was his house. "If I wanted," Ernie thought, "I could stomp downstairs, flop on the sofa, and fire up Asteroid Attack, level nine!" Level nine was for the real experts. It was the most action-packed and noisiest Asteroid Attack of them all. "I could sit there and fight asteroids and listen from the same room if I wanted," Ernie reasoned, "so I can listen from upstairs."

However, the task of listening from upstairs was trickier

than it seemed. Ernie tried listening through the floor in his bedroom but he couldn't understand a thing. He tried the heating vent in the hall but all he could hear was the low murmur of wind in the vents and a soft clicking as the furnace turned on and off. Ernie went into the bathroom and tried pressing his ear against the pipes. That worked a little better—he almost heard voices—but the pipes made his ears too cold. Ernie was about to give up altogether when, quite suddenly, he heard the last thing he ever expected to hear.

It was music.

In the living room, Cat Lady poked through the bookshelves while Red figured out the controls to the stereo. "I used to know how to work this thing," Red said.

"Are you a reader?" Cat Lady asked, running her hand over the books.

"I was a reader," said Red, "but not so much anymore. Magazines and newspapers mostly. History books, sometimes. Biographies."

Cat Lady plucked a biography of Charles Lindbergh from the shelf. "Have you read this?" she asked.

At the same moment, Red got the stereo to work. The speakers sputtered and crackled slightly as though music had not poured out of them in some time. Even then, what emerged was not the kind of music that Red ever listened to in the car. It sounded more like elevator music.

Red smiled, fully prepared to take credit for inventing the stereo—and Cat Lady held out the book. As she did, a small piece of paper fell from its pages. It danced briefly in the air, grazed off the sofa, and fluttered to the ground. Cat Lady bent down to pick the paper off the carpet. "What do you know?" she said. "Another note."

Red looked at her curiously. "Another what?"

Cat Lady raised the paper between her fingers. "I found a note in the kitchen when I was watching Ernie," she said. "It said, 'Eat your peas.'" She turned the note over to read the words. "This one says 'Tag, you're it,'" she said. "What does that mean?"

Red took the note. "My wife liked to leave notes around the house," he explained. "It's been more than a year since we lost her but I still find them from time to time. I guess they're for me or for Ernie or for anyone who finds them."

Red sat down on the sofa and tapped the note against his palm. It was suddenly quiet and unexpectedly awkward between them as though Cat Lady had unintentionally knocked some small thing off the shelf and it had silently shattered into a hundred pieces. Neither of them spoke for a long moment.

Red reached to store the note on the end table but he couldn't seem to find anywhere to put it. Before he could speak, Cat Lady sighed, waved her arms absently in the air, and abruptly reached for her bag. "Maybe I should go," she said.

"No," Red blurted, rising to his feet. They were standing much closer than either of them expected. Neither of them moved. "No reason to go," said Red. He took Cat Lady's hand and, quite unexpectedly, began to sway to the music.

It is impossible to say how long Ernie had been watching from the upstairs landing. He was hiding behind the banister, hardly hidden at all, and peering past the archway. It was an awkward angle but he could glimpse enough to follow Red and Cat Lady in the living room. He couldn't actually hear what they were saying but he knew what he saw.

Cat Lady and Red were dancing.

CHAPTER TWELVE

The Wrong Gloves

Swimming Pool had high hopes of scoring a home run at charm school. Her first impression had been a little bumpy and she thought if she were on time, attentive, and prepared, she might repair the damage.

Unfortunately, nothing is ever easy. Swimming Pool was scheduled for charm school that afternoon, but her mom had to work late at the post office so her dad was doing the afternoon run and that meant loading the van to drop one brother at kickboxing, another at tai kwan do, another at football, and Swimming Pool at charm. For some reason, they also had to deliver a tuba to band practice.

"I don't get it. Who plays the tuba?" Swimming Pool's dad shouted to the van full of kids.

"Nobody," Swimming Pool grumbled as she laced up

her sneakers beneath the dashboard. "It doesn't matter," she said. "We still have to drop it."

With the unexpected delay due to the brothers and the tuba, Swimming Pool had about one minute before she was late to charm school. She cringed at the thought. "Hurry, Dad, hurry," Swimming Pool said, as she tugged on the collar on her blue dress with the duck. "This is too close for comfort!"

Swimming Pool's father bounced on the brakes when he stopped the van in front of Miss Ginger's School of Tap & Tumbling. He seemed to enjoy making Swimming Pool squirm. Swimming Pool threw herself from the van and was just about to slam the van door when she realized—she wasn't wearing any gloves. Miss Ginger was a stickler for lateness but she was an even bigger stickler for gloves.

"My gloves, my gloves!" Swimming Pool cried, diving back into the van in a panic. "I forgot my gloves!" She crawled over her brothers and past the tuba until she arrived at the way-back of the van. She reached into the plastic bin that held their sporting equipment, which is where she usually chucked her gloves after charm school, and started digging. She was frantically tossing shin guards and face masks right and left—but she wasn't finding her gloves.

"Who took them?" Swimming Pool yelled. "Who took my gloves?"

Her brothers hooted and cackled. "I took them!" said one. "I threw them in the garbage!" said another. Swimming Pool's brothers loved to see her upset.

"Cut it out, you goons," Swimming Pool's father

barked. He eyed Swimming Pool in the rearview mirror. "What are you doing back there?" he asked, with more curiosity than concern.

"Gloves!" Swimming Pool cried. "I need gloves!" She made it sound like a medical emergency.

"Well, you left two right here on the front seat," her father replied.

"Why didn't you say so?" Swimming Pool yelled. With a grunt and a groan, she put herself into reverse and backed through the van, over her brothers and under the tuba, until she reached the front seat.

Her father turned his cheek as though Swimming Pool wasn't going anywhere or getting anything until she delivered a kiss. Swimming Pool grunted with exasperation, smooched her father's cheek, and grabbed the gloves from his hand. Then she hopped out of the van, slammed the van door, and ran like mad for charm school.

Somehow Swimming Pool managed to be sitting in formation with the other girls when Miss Ginger entered the room. She was still catching her breath and panting like a puppy because, as she had later boasted to Betty, "I made it from the parking lot to my seat in fifteen flat!" As soon as Swimming Pool collapsed in her seat, Miss Ginger hit the door.

"Good afternoon, Miss Ginger," the girls chimed, in a singsong chorus. They were all perched upright with their ankles delicately crossed, their heads tilted, and their hands clasped, one palm on top of the other.

"Oh, my!" said Miss Ginger, smiling in pleasant surprise.

She had spent the last class session instructing the girls on the proper way to sit. It had been a difficult hour. "Well!" she exclaimed. "I'm glad to see our last visit at charm school wasn't completely—!"

Miss Ginger never finished that sentence. She dropped the thought altogether in her haste to swoop down the row of seats and descend upon Swimming Pool.

"Good afternoon, Miss Ginger," Swimming Pool repeated, in the same singsong manner.

"Swimming Pool!" Miss Ginger snapped, glaring down at her. Swimming Pool couldn't imagine what she had done wrong. Her "Good afternoon, Miss Ginger" was every bit as cheerful as the other girls'.

That was when Swimming Pool realized that she was hunched forward in her chair like she was sitting in the dugout. She eased herself upright and slid her shoulders back. But still Miss Ginger was glaring.

"I guess I didn't fix the right problem," Swimming Pool thought, holding her position and rolling her eyeballs until she located something else wrong. It was then that Swimming Pool noticed that her red high-tops were wrapped around the legs of the chair. She adjusted her feet until they matched the other girls', gently crossed at the ankle. But Miss Ginger was still glaring.

Swimming Pool could not imagine what else she had done wrong. She raised a hand to scratch her head, hoping that might jump-start the thinking process—and that was when the problem struck Swimming Pool in the face. She was wearing the wrong gloves. The other girls were wearing the dainty, white, standard-issue, wrist-length specials.

Swimming Pool had an outfielder's glove on her left hand and a catcher's mitt on her right.

"Um, good afternoon, Miss Ginger," Swimming Pool repeated timidly.

"If this is supposed to be a joke," Miss Ginger snapped, "I don't think it's very funny."

"I didn't exactly mean for it to be a joke," said Swimming Pool. "I just knew I had to have gloves."

Miss Ginger sighed. Her patience was wearing thin. "Swimming Pool," she said with an air of self-sacrifice, "I have tried to teach you how to behave like a proper young lady and still you insist on pulling these unseemly stunts."

"It wasn't intentional," Swimming Pool protested.

"Whoosh!" cried Miss Ginger. Swimming Pool had been whooshed so often during charm school that Miss Ginger shorthanded the reprimand to one single whoosh. "Today's lesson has yet to begin," Miss Ginger announced to the assembled girls, "and already Swimming Pool is pulling a technical strike two." Miss Ginger held up two fingers in a V-sign. Swimming Pool lowered her head in shame.

"Please, Miss Ginger," she said. "It wasn't on purpose, I swear."

Miss Ginger waved her hands. The matter was closed. "Go to my office," she instructed, "and retrieve a pair of emergency gloves from my desk drawer."

"Yes, ma'am, Miss Ginger," said Swimming Pool.

"And take those baseball gloves with you," Miss Ginger added. "I don't want those awful things in the room."

"Yes, ma'am," Swimming Pool repeated. She took off the wrong gloves and slumped out of the room with her head appropriately lowered in shame.

In truth, Swimming Pool was more frustrated than ashamed. Maybe she wasn't meant for charm school. No matter how hard she tried, she always did the wrong thing. And if she was being honest with herself, charm school hadn't turned out to be anything like Swimming Pool thought it would be. She was giving serious thought to bagging the whole ordeal. Even if it meant bagging baseball at the same time.

She had said as much to Dusty the day before in his kitchen. Dusty had pulled his daily batch of peanut butter cookies out of the oven and was setting them on the rack to cool. "I'm ready to bag it, Dusty," said Swimming Pool. "You don't know. Charm school is harder than you'd think."

Dusty slid a single cookie onto the breadboard in front of Swimming Pool. "Careful," he said, "it's hot."

"Thanks," Swimming Pool said, placing a hand over the cookie to test its warmth.

"I don't know," Dusty surmised, thoughtfully. "I know how much you like baseball. And I think you like charm school more than you let on."

"What's that supposed to mean?" asked Swimming Pool. Her voice sounded kind of garbled because she was balancing a two-finger pinch of peanut butter cookie on the end of her tongue, hoping it would cool.

"You've been different since you started charm school," said Dusty. "I've noticed. It's like you think twice before you fly off the handle. You don't yell nearly so much. And I can't remember the last time you punched me in the head."

"Whoosh-whoosh-whoosh," said Swimming Pool, waving her hand in front of her face. "I never punched you in the head."

"You did that one time, but it was an accident," said Dusty. Then he tapped his forehead like he had the memory of an elephant.

"You're making this up," said Swimming Pool. "If I ever punched you in the head, I would have apologized."

"That's what I'm talking about," said Dusty. "Apologizing for a punch in the head. The old Swimming Pool would never have apologized for a punch in the head. You would have said, 'Get over it, crybaby.' Which is what you said when you punched me in the head, but I've already forgiven you so let's forget about it."

Swimming Pool pursed her lips and tilted her head thoughtfully. Maybe Dusty was right. "You really think I'm changing?" she asked.

"No doubt about it," said Dusty.

Swimming Pool slipped into Miss Ginger's tiny office in search of her emergency gloves. The place was pretty much a dump. It was worse than Swimming Pool's room and that was pretty bad. Miss Ginger's desk was piled with stacks of paper, boxes, and magazines. The floor was strewn with shoeboxes and tutus. "Oh great," Swimming Pool groaned. "How am I going to find the emergency gloves in this mess?" She tugged open the desk drawer. It was full of pencils and paper clips. There were no gloves to be found.

At that moment, Finny and Fanny happened to walk

past the door with two tall, teetering stacks of books. "Hey, Finny and Fanny," Swimming Pool said, "have you girls got a clue where Miss Ginger keeps her emergency gloves?"

"Try the deep drawer," said Finny.

"Yeah," added Fanny, "that's where she keeps the emergency tap shoes."

"Thanks," said Swimming Pool. She pulled open the deep drawer and sure enough, there were the emergency gloves. Standard issue, cotton, white. They were knotted up in a heap of ribbons, shoelaces, and loose socks next to the first-aid kit.

Swimming Pool slid the emergency gloves over her fingers. She still didn't know why gloves were mandatory in charm school but when she saw how nice they looked on her hand, she thought maybe she could live with the mystery of it all. "I've survived worse," she thought. "Compared to catechism, charm school is a piece of cake."

She bumped the deep drawer shut with her hip and scurried out of the office. She was hoping to glide back into charm school as seamlessly as possible. Maybe that would make a good impression on Miss Ginger. When she reached the doorway, however, she caught sight of something that stopped her cold in her tracks. It's a good thing Miss Ginger didn't notice because Swimming Pool's mouth was hanging wide open.

The girls were in the middle of the studio, trying to walk in a straight line, except it really wasn't very straight at all. It had more curves than a caterpillar, a conga line, or a Chinese dragon. The girls were all stepping gingerly, wobbling on their feet and wagging their outstretched arms like the Flying

Wallenda Family doing a tightrope walk at the circus.

That was when Swimming Pool realized what was going on. Each girl was balancing a book on her head.

Swimming Pool covered her mouth with a glove to stifle a giggle. "Oh, I'm in," she thought. "Miss Ginger has outdone herself! Charm school is out of control! I wouldn't miss this for the world!"

CHAPTER THIRTEEN

My Favorite Book

Miss Ginger motioned for Swimming Pool to stay where she was while the girls struggled to maintain their balance with the books. Swimming Pool was happy to stand back because, frankly, it looked a little perilous. The books bobbed precariously, listing from side to side on the girls' heads while their faces fretted and frowned beneath. The whole mass of girls warbled and wobbled.

Betty inched forward fearfully like she was on her first bike with no training wheels. Gina looked solemn and grim as if she'd been asked to walk the plank. Finny and Fanny, twins to the core, had their eyes locked on each other's teetering book with little regard for their own. Kirsten was doing a better balancing job than most girls, except that her voice kept a running commentary that betrayed her certainty that her book would fall.

"Woo-woo-woo-woo—!" Kirsten piped. "It's gonna fall, gonna fall, gonna fall—"

And then it did. Kirsten lurched to catch the book in midair—but that effort only started a chain reaction that ran in either direction like a stack of dominoes. Books flew right and left and the girls began to tumble to the floor. The room was filled with screams and squeals as a veritable library fell from the sky.

Miss Ginger was apparently already prepared for that result. Her gloved hands had been planted firmly over her ears. She didn't even move them as she uttered a single word. "Whoosh."

Swimming Pool stepped closer as the girls descended to the floor, trying to reclaim their book, or, hopefully snag a lighter volume.

"Nice try, Kirsten," Swimming Pool offered with a friendly smile.

"Well, what do you expect?" Kirsten snarled, taking the game a little too seriously. "I was stuck with a stinking encyclopedia!"

"Any book will do!" Miss Ginger chimed above the fray. The situation had become slightly chaotic.

When the girls finally resumed their line, each partici-pant stood with both arms wrapped protectively around her book. In half-whispers, the girls compared book titles the way convicts compare sentences. "I got *Jane Eyre*," Betty told Kirsten. "What'd you get?"

"I got the thesaurus," Kirsten answered with a sulk and

a hiss. Betty groaned. The thesaurus was cruel and unusual punishment.

Miss Ginger handed a book to Swimming Pool and ushered her into line. Swimming Pool flipped over the cover to see the title. "*Little Women*," she read aloud. "Oh, brother. Am I supposed to read this thing?"

"We don't read them, we wear them," Betty corrected.

Swimming Pool made a face as if to say, "This is the wackiest class I have ever taken!"

"And this is supposed to teach us—what?" she asked with a laugh.

Betty and Kirsten were still caught up in the competition. "We don't ask," said Kirsten. "We just do as we're told."

Betty jerked her head toward the girl at the head of the line. "Can you believe that girl?" she sneered. "No fair. Pigtail advantage."

Gina briskly rubbed the cover of *Anne of Green Gables* and tried to screw it to her head.

"You think that's gonna help?" asked Swimming Pool.

"Friction works with a balloon," said Gina.

"All right, girls," offered Miss Ginger in soothing tones, lifting *The Doctors Wives' Cookbook* over her head. "Position your volume over the crown of your head!"

Swimming Pool watched as the other girls moved their books into position. This balancing act was a recipe for disaster. "There's got to be an easier way," thought Swimming Pool. Maybe if she found a way to balance the book on her head so that she could still get across the room, she might regain some lost ground with Miss Ginger.

"Swimming Pool," Miss Ginger intoned, "are you going to join us or not?"

"Yes, ma'am!" Swimming Pool began to place the book on her head like all the other girls—but then she had a sudden brainstorm. "Eureka!" she cried. She flipped her book over and opened it to the center. She boldly stepped out of line, certain that Miss Ginger was going to be really pleased.

"Swimming Pool, back in line, please," Miss Ginger said.

"Hold it. You're going to like this. I mean it," Swimming Pool said with enthusiasm. She lifted the book overhead and let it drape from her ears like a pup tent. That way, she could twist her head from side to side and the book stayed in place. It looked stupid, of course—but they all looked stupid anyway.

"How's this, huh? 'Look, Ma! No Hands!'" Swimming Pool cried. She had solved the puzzle and fixed the trick.

Unfortunately, her stunt had exactly the opposite effect. The girls shrieked with laughter at the sight of Swimming Pool with the book draped over her ears. Miss Ginger hissed, "Swimming Pool," and leveled a gloved finger like an indictment. "Explain to me how this isn't a technical strike three."

Swimming Pool was crestfallen. She drooped her head in disappointment. Little Women slid off her head and she caught it before it hit the ground. She returned to the line and did her best to balance the book on her head the way the other girls were—but it was much harder than it sounds.

"We're not supposed to walk around in public like this, are we?" Swimming Pool groused to the other girls.

Betty clamped her hand on top of her book like she was

wearing a hat in the wind. "Swimming Pool," she said, "we already know it's stupid. I think we're just supposed to try."

Swimming Pool shrugged. She wasn't afraid to try. She joined the ranks of girls as they inched forward, ducking and dodging each other to pick up their books when they went crashing to the floor.

"Now I know why boys get out of charm school," Swimming Pool muttered to Gina. "It takes too much coordination." She wiggled like a hula dancer, trying to keep *Little Women* from slipping off her head—but it fell anyway. It whacked the floor with a loud thunk and fell open so that the pages flapped from side to side.

When Swimming Pool bent down to retrieve the book, she happened to notice the chapter illustration at the top of a page. It was a drawing of a finger pressed against a pair of lips and the chapter title read "Beth's Secret."

"Hmm, Beth's got a secret," thought Swimming Pool. Her curiosity got the better of her. She skimmed the first paragraph of the chapter, figuring she could get to Beth's secret without much bother—but by the end of the page, she still hadn't figured out what was going on. "What is this book about?" Swimming Pool wondered.

She put the volume back on top of her head and tried to do the balancing act again. Miss Ginger was monitoring the room so Swimming Pool felt like she had to put on a good show.

Even so, Swimming Pool found that she couldn't stop thinking about "Beth's Secret." So she let the book fall off her head again, bent over to pick it up, and hurriedly flipped through the pages, trying to get back to the same spot. She couldn't find "Beth's Secret" but she did stumble across a different chapter titled "Castles in the Air." That sounded intriguing and it only made her more curious about "Beth's Secret."

Swimming Pool groaned in frustration. "I'm just going to have to start this book from the top," she said. So she put the book back on top of her head and let it fall again so that she could flip to the beginning and get started. It didn't take long before Swimming Pool was hooked.

By this point, Miss Ginger expected the girls to be running drills back and forth across the room with their books perfectly balanced. "No excuses! Look at me!" she cried, gliding effortlessly across the room with a book on her head. "I can do it! And this is the Doctor's Wives Cookbook!"

Some of the girls were actually making progress. They had the hang of balancing a book on their heads and were crisscrossing the room with relative ease. Other girls had given up on the exercise and were totally faking it. Technically, Swimming Pool could be listed in the latter camp but, in truth, she was also happily plowing through the first chapters of Little Women.

Swimming Pool had discovered that if she hooked a finger between the pages, she didn't lose her place in Little Women when she had to pretend the book had fallen off her head. She was also in the habit of retreating to the corners so that she could hide behind another girl and get to the end of a paragraph without being interrupted.

"Swimming Pool," said Gina when she saw her with her nose buried in the book. "What are you doing?"

"Has anybody read this thing?" Swimming Pool asked, holding her book on display.

"*Little Women?*" said Kirsten, with a look that suggested that Swimming Pool must be out of her mind.

"No, I'm serious," Swimming Pool whispered. "This book is good!" She pointed at the cover and raised a big thumbs-up. "I can't get enough! I can't put it down!"

Miss Ginger was headed their way so the girls ducked back under their books and grimaced as they struggled for balance.

When Miss Ginger finally signaled that the exercise was at an end, Kirsten let her thesaurus fall with a heavy thunk. "Ah, freedom!" she cried. Across the room, girls issued heavy sighs and let their books whack the floor. It was quitting time on a chain gang.

Swimming Pool was the only girl who groaned with disappointment. She was also the only girl left with a book in her hands. Betty threw Swimming Pool a look as if to say, "Are you out of your mind?" But Swimming Pool hugged *Little Women* to her chest as if she couldn't bear to let it go. "I swear this is my new favorite book!" she said.

Miss Ginger clapped her hands to make an announcement. "Next week, I have a special surprise," she said. The girls held their breath—and not in delight. After today's drill with the books, they couldn't imagine what Miss Ginger had up her sleeve.

"Next week, we're going to hold a little dance competition," Miss Ginger continued with great excitement. The girls rustled uncertainly. By this point, they didn't know whether to trust Miss Ginger or not.

"Nothing too technical," Miss Ginger assured them after reading their discomfort. "Just a little game I like to play. But there are prizes!"

"What kind of prizes?" asked Betty.

"Silver dollars," Miss Ginger replied with relish and an air of mystery. Some girls warmed to the idea. They cooed at the lavishness of it all.

"And," Miss Ginger continued, prolonging the word as if an extra-special announcement were to follow. She left the girls hanging in a moment of suspense. "And," Miss Ginger repeated, "I am hoping that there will be boys."

At the very utterance of the single word—boys—the room erupted into a state of hysteria that Swimming Pool had never known. Miss Ginger allowed the excitement to build through a natural arc before she even attempted to bring order to the room.

Swimming Pool was perplexed. "What's the big deal with boys?" Swimming Pool muttered to Gina. "I know plenty of boys. My entire family is full of boys."

Before Gina could respond, Miss Ginger resumed her announcement. "I have extended an invitation to a number of boys in our tumbling, modeling, and karate classes here at Miss Ginger's. But I also want to encourage you to extend an invitation to any little friend you might want to bring along."

The girls hooted and tittered with enthusiasm as though Miss Ginger had just issued a challenge.

Swimming Pool was still confused. She raised her hand for an opportunity to speak. "Are the boys going to have to do the thing with books on their heads?" she asked. "Because I don't think boys can really do that."

Swimming Pool thought her question was perfectly reasonable but the room still burst into laughter.

"No, Swimming Pool," said Miss Ginger dismissively. "Don't be so silly! The boys won't be here to wear books on their heads. The boys will be here to dance."

"But—" Swimming Pool hesitated, but then she went ahead. "I don't think many boys know how to dance either." It seemed as if Swimming Pool couldn't open her mouth without causing the room to burst into laughter.

Miss Ginger smiled knowingly. "Boys who can't dance don't make very good dance partners," she said. "So I encourage you bring a boy who can dance. Or at least one who can fake it."

Gina raised her hand. "Can we bring our little brothers?"

Miss Ginger looked slightly disappointed but she permitted the exception. "That's not really rising to the challenge but I will allow little brothers, yes."

When charm school was dismissed, Swimming Pool felt obliged to stay behind to ask Miss Ginger a question.

"I thought so," Miss Ginger said with a smile. "A question about boys?"

"No," said Swimming Pool. "It's about *Little Women*." She held up her copy of the book. "I want to get better at the balancing thing and also I want to get to the end. So can

I borrow this? It's a pretty thick book."

Miss Ginger took a moment to look at Swimming Pool and let out a long, slow sigh. "You're not very happy at charm school, are you, Swimming Pool?"

Swimming Pool was stumped. "Are you kidding me?" she cried. "I love charm school! I haven't skipped once!"

Miss Ginger looked concerned. "Then how do you explain your attitude?" she said.

"My attitude?" Swimming Pool repeated. "I didn't know I had one."

Miss Ginger crossed her arms and threw her shoulders back. "I'm talking about the burping, the baseball gloves, the book on your head," she said. "Don't think I didn't notice strike two and strike three. Technically, you struck out today, Swimming Pool. It's official."

Swimming Pool's jaw dropped and her eyes got wide. She felt a lump in her throat as if she really needed a water fountain. "Oh no, Miss Ginger," was all she could say.

Miss Ginger shook her head from side to side like there was nothing more to be said. "I'm not interested in excuses," she continued. "My hands are tied. I have every right to call you out."

Swimming Pool's shoulders dropped and her heart sank. "Please, Miss Ginger," she said. "You don't mean it."

Miss Ginger tugged off her gloves and tossed them on the desk. She sighed once and looked at Swimming Pool. "Correct me if I'm wrong, Swimming Pool, but you treat everything like a great big joke."

Swimming Pool didn't know what to say. She was one of the most serious and responsible girls she knew, except for a few eccentricities. How could she defend herself against someone who thought she was a joke? And how did Miss Ginger get that idea? "That's not true, Miss Ginger," she said. "I'm not like that at all."

"Mmm-hmm," said Miss Ginger and that was all she said.

Swimming Pool was fairly stumped. She stammered for a moment. "I'm sorry, I'll try harder," is what came out of her mouth. It was her tried-and-true excuse at school and it seemed to work well for any occasion.

"I'm happy to hear that, Swimming Pool, but I'm not entirely convinced. I have students who want to learn charm. And I'm not going to let you stand in their way. Is that clear, Swimming Pool?"

Swimming Pool still didn't understand. "Are you throwing me out of charm school?" she asked. She could feel her pulse racing as she waited for the answer.

Miss Ginger didn't say yes and she didn't say no. Instead, she said, "I wouldn't want to have to throw anyone out of charm school. I think the better question is whether you really want to be here."

Swimming Pool was still trying to figure out what had happened with Miss Ginger as she waited on the curb for her dad to pick her up in the van. She certainly didn't feel welcome in charm school but at the same time, she couldn't say that Miss Ginger had tried to make her quit. "What the heck was that about?" Swimming Pool wondered.

Only one thing was clear. Swimming Pool had to rise to the challenge and ask a boy to that dance contest.

But who?

CHAPTER FOURTEEN

Good Morning

As the week settled into another cool, clear, crisp Saturday morning, kids across the neighborhood peered into cupboards and pondered the cereal selection. Bowls and spoons clattered onto counters and milk cartons went "glug-glug-glug." Many kids had already flopped in front of the television to motor through the cartoon lineup with the remote control.

It was a typical Saturday morning.

But not for Dusty. Nothing in the world would have made Dusty happier than to curl up on the carpet with corn puffs and cartoons. But that wasn't going to happen this Saturday morning. This Saturday was different.

Dusty was on a mission.

Dusty hadn't planned on a completely different Saturday when he awoke just before dawn. He looked out the window and the purple sky had barely started to lighten. He had slept well enough. No nightmares, no boogie men, no monsters in the closet. But the moment Dusty woke, he had automatically started worrying about the ballpark.

Dusty had been worrying about the ballpark ever since he and Ernie scored free paint from the Moose Lodge. They ended up with an odd smattering of leftover blue, gray, yellow, lime green, and an unlikely pink. Ernie wouldn't turn any of it down.

"Beggars can't be choosers," Ernie said.

"Sure," said Dusty, trying to be positive. "It's a challenge but I can work with these colors." Dusty had been trying to stay on Ernie's good side. He harbored hopes that if he did a good job on the ballpark, he and Ernie would be thick as thieves again.

Unfortunately, Dusty still didn't have a plan for the ballpark. More than a week had passed and those paint cans were still stacked in the Comets' dugout. The ballpark was still a wreck. Ernie had begun saying things like, "Any day now, Dusty!" and the Comets had started to complain about having to sit on all those cans.

In the old days, Dusty could get his creative juices going by having a powwow with Ernie and Swimming Pool. They used to bounce ideas back and forth. It was a lot of fun. But these days, Ernie and Swimming Pool were too busy for Dusty. These days, Ernie and Swimming Pool had new friends.

Dusty flung back the covers. He went to the bathroom

to brush his teeth and then he headed downstairs for a peanut butter cookie. His mother claimed that cookies weren't a breakfast food but she wasn't awake yet.

He could have turned on the television in the kitchen without waking his parents—but instead he flopped onto the sofa to eat his cookie with his head poking through the curtains covering the living-room window. Usually Dusty slept through the sunrise. But he remembered that his dad always said, "It's free and it's the best show in town!" Dusty thought he'd check it out.

Between nibbles, Dusty watched as long, flat clouds stretched across the sky, turning red, yellow, and orange. The sun itself had yet to clear the tract houses and factories along the horizon but the sky was going crazy with color. It was a new day.

It suddenly occurred to Dusty that "If I took one new day, sunrise to sunset, and thought about the ballpark and only the ballpark and nothing but the ballpark, I'm sure I'd have a bright idea by sundown. I could just do that today. I could just get off this sofa and do that today."

When Dusty arrived at the ballpark, the ground was still damp with dew. The Comets wouldn't arrive for several hours. He dropped his bike on the grass and hiked over the diamond to perch cross-legged smack in the middle of the pitcher's mound. Dusty hadn't spent much time on the pitcher's mound. Usually if he needed to talk to Swimming Pool, he used their sign language from home plate.

He turned his back on home plate to face the outfield. The sun was barely peeking over the horizon now and still putting on quite a show over the outfield fence.

But that fence was the big problem. Dusty needed to paint something spectacular on the fence. It was the focal point of the ballpark.

"Why don't I just whitewash the whole thing and be done with it?" Dusty muttered to himself. "Tell the team, 'Here you go—a white fence, hope you like it.'"

But if he had tried that idea in a powwow, Ernie would have said, "Dust-man, get out of here." Swimming Pool would have said, "White paint? Am I hearing right? Did you say white paint?"

Or, at least, that's what Dusty imagined.

"One good idea," he thought, "and my job is done. Everything else will fall into place." It was as if all the bright ideas were stuck inside his head, filling up on corn puffs and cartoons and refusing to come out and play. Dusty grunted. It would be so much easier if he could bounce ideas off Swimming Pool and Ernie but that wasn't going to happen.

"All right, then," Dusty thought. "Be that way. I'm going to sit on the pitcher's mound and watch that fence like a television and I'm not gonna budge until that bright idea comes."

After fifteen minutes, the fence still looked like a fence. Dusty still hadn't had a single idea. His legs got sore and his mind started to wander. "The fence, the fence," thought Dusty. "I'm not thinking about Ernie and Swimming Pool anymore."

But even though he tried not to, sometimes he did.

Of course, it was more than a little weird when, a couple hours later, the Comets began to show up for practice and found Dusty planted on the pitcher's mound.

"Hey, Dusty, what's up?" asked one of the big kids. Dusty was shocked to hear his name out loud. He didn't think the big kids even knew his name.

Ronjon and Marcus stood over Dusty at the pitcher's mound. "What are you doing, Dusty?" asked Ronjon.

"Figuring something out," said Dusty, looking back to the fence.

Ronjon and Marcus exchanged a glance. "Figuring what out?" said Marcus.

"How to paint the outfield fence," said Dusty. "I have to come up with a new ballpark."

Ronjon arched an eyebrow. "Well, I'll help you paint it, if you need help," he said. "I'm a good painter."

"That's okay," said Dusty. "I don't need any help. Thanks, anyway."

"You sure?" said Ronjon. "I can slap a couple coats up there in no time."

"I'm kind of particular about paint," said Dusty. "But thanks anyway."

Ronjon and Marcus nodded okay, like everything was absolutely normal. But when they got to the dugout, they turned back to notice that Dusty was still sitting on the pitcher's mound.

"Is he going to sit on the pitcher's mound all through practice?" asked Marcus.

Ronjon made the universal sound for "I dunno."

Not long after that, Ernie arrived on the scene and asked the same question. "What's up with Dusty?" Ernie asked. "Is he going to sit on the pitcher's mound all through practice?"

Ronjon, Marcus, and Chuck made the universal sound for "I dunno."

Ernie walked out to the pitcher's mound and stood directly in front of Dusty, deliberately blocking his view of the outfield fence.

"Um, Dusty," he said. "Good morning."

"Good morning," said Dusty.

"Good morning," said Ernie. "Um, we're about to start practice. Last time I checked, you were still on the team. You're still our catcher. Are you planning to sit on the pitcher's mound the whole time we're holding practice?"

Dusty didn't say anything.

Ernie continued. "I'm only asking because we're here for baseball practice and—just so you know, there are going to be baseballs flying all over the place out here." Ernie waited for a reaction.

"Go ahead," said Dusty. "Play ball."

Ernie stood back and studied Dusty on the mound. Then he leaned a little closer. His voice shifted with concern. "Dusty, what are you doing?" he asked.

"I'm working on the design," said Dusty. "I'm coming up with a new ballpark."

"Can't you, like, do that in your head?"

"I'm trying to get out of my head," Dusty insisted. "That's why I've been sitting here since dawn."

"You've been sitting here since dawn?" Ernie couldn't believe this was happening.

"And I'm going to keep sitting here until I figure out this ballpark," said Dusty.

Ernie looked away and sighed. Dusty had exhausted Ernie's patience with his artistic temperament.

Over at the dugout, the Comets were dangling from the chain-link fence like monkeys at the zoo. Ernie figured they were all waiting to see the outcome of his showdown. Ernie wouldn't admit it, but he felt that his leadership was being called into question.

"Well, okay," said Ernie, turning back to Dusty. "Sit on the pitcher's mound all day." He made it sound like it was perfectly reasonable until he added with a slight snarl, "Just don't come crying to me when you get hit by the ball."

"I've been hit by the ball before," answered Dusty. "Plenty of times. Don't worry about me. I'll be fine."

Ernie looked down at Dusty on the pitcher's mound. He screwed up his lips like there was something he could say but he didn't want to say it—and then he did. "Um, no. You're not fine. I'm worried about you, Dusty, because you're acting weird."

"Weird?"

"Different. Weird. Like, the whole peanut butter cookie thing. Every day you're making peanut butter cookies," said Ernie. "Here on planet Earth, that's weird."

"They're good," said Dusty. "In case you didn't notice." Dusty was proud of his peanut butter cookies.

"But you make them every day, Dusty," Ernie said, getting a little shrill. "It's like an obsession or something. It's weird!"

"You don't have to eat them," Dusty said, looking down.

Ernie sighed. He didn't want to cut off his supply of cookies. "I only said it's weird."

"I heard you before," said Dusty. He shifted uncomfortably.

"And now you wanna sit on the pitcher's mound while we practice? I dunno, Dusty, it's—" Ernie looked up at the sky as if he couldn't find the words.

"I know," said Dusty. "I'm *weird*."

Ernie waved his arms helplessly like there was no sense discussing this anymore. "Dusty, I need to know. I have the team depending on me. I have to run practice. Are you going to sit on the mound all through practice?"

"Yes," said Dusty, in a perfect sulk. "I'm on a mission. I'm not going to budge."

Ernie turned on his heel, muttering to himself, and walked back to the dugout.

Kip was waiting in the dugout when Ernie arrived. "Okay," Kip said with a cheerful shrug. "I give. Dusty, pitcher's mound. What's the story?"

The whole team made the universal sound for "I dunno."

"He says he's on a mission," said Ernie.

"A *what?*" said Kip.

Ernie kicked the fence with his foot. Then, without another word, he lifted his head toward the team and hollered, "Let's play ball!"

It was awkward at first, but somehow the team managed to play a practice game while Dusty remained seated on the mound. Marcus scored a double off a fly ball. Chuck snagged a triple play. And Dusty still managed to sit there, concentrating—or trying to concentrate—as the ball rolled, flew, or bounced past him and players ran this way and that.

It was almost a normal practice.

Then—at some point between the fifth and sixth innings, just as everyone had gotten accustomed to Dusty sitting there—Dusty did this strange thing.

He stood up.

He stood up and brushed himself off and then he walked toward the outfield fence.

The Comets were still involved in the game but it became increasingly distracting to keep their eyes on the ball—and still keep one eye on what Dusty was doing.

When Dusty reached the fence, he pulled a piece of chalk out of his pocket and began long arcing lines all over the outfield wall. He'd place the chalk in position and then hold it there as he took a long stroll to the opposite foul line. Then he'd reposition the chalk at another point on the wall and start the long walk back.

Clearly, Dusty was up to something—and it looked as if he'd finally had a bright idea. Later on, Dusty said it came to him in two simple words: *Good morning.* "And the funny thing was," said Dusty, "I'd been staring at it the whole entire time."

When a line drive sailed past Ronjon and into the outfield, he had the perfect excuse to trot next to Dusty and take a closer look at the fence. The ball bounced off the wood but Dusty didn't seem distracted in the least. Ronjon scooped up the ball, heaved it toward the infield, and trailed Dusty for a while.

"I wanna help," said Ronjon, after a moment or two.

"I don't really need any help," said Dusty. "But thanks. I prefer to do it by myself."

Ronjon hustled to stay in step with Dusty as he continued his chalkline. "I could get the paint," Ronjon offered. "I'm a really good painter."

"You said that before," said Dusty. "But, really, I'm kind of particular about paint so—I'm fine. I can do this by myself."

"But it's a really big fence," Ronjon protested.

Before Dusty could raise another objection, Noah Morgenstern came running into the outfield with a can of paint.

"I brought the paint," said Noah.

"I'm not ready for the paint," said Dusty. "I still have to finish the drawing part."

"What are you making?" said Marcus, backing about as far off second base as a second base player should go.

"I offered to help, but he said no," Ronjon explained to Marcus.

"Why not?" said Marcus. "We got lots of brushes."

"Thanks, but no thanks," said Dusty. "I got this idea in my head and I know what I want and it's probably best if I just do the whole thing by myself."

"This is our fence too," said Ronjon. "We should be able to help."

Dusty looked up to see that Chuck and Larry were running from the dugout to the outfield, and they were both carrying paint cans. It looked like everyone on the team was determined to help.

Dusty put his foot down. "Look, look, look," he said, holding up his hands and feeling overwhelmed. "I can do this by myself."

"Why not let us help?" said Ronjon.

Dusty didn't have an answer for that question. He

looked over their faces. He knew they were basically nice guys. He just didn't know all their names yet.

"Okay, look," said Dusty. "I'll let you help paint but I'm really particular about paint so you have to let me choose the colors."

Everybody nodded like that was no problem.

Dusty hedged slightly because the next question was a little sensitive. "And I cannot let you paint unless you can stay between the lines. How many of you guys can stay between the lines?"

Most of the Comets raised their hands. Noah Morgenstern raised his hand but then he lowered it because everybody knew he couldn't stay between the lines.

"Okay," said Dusty, jumping into action. "I'm gonna break this down like paint-by-numbers." He jumped between the paint cans, assigning a code to the colors. "One is for blue, two is for gray, three is for yellow." When he finished with the cans, he began assigning those same numbers to different chalk sections on the fence.

The Comets tossed their gloves into the grass, grabbed cans and brushes, and spread out along the wall, waiting for further instructions. When Dusty gave the go-ahead, they dipped brushes into the cans and began to slop paint on the wooden slats.

"Long even strokes," Dusty cried. "Remember, you promised! Long even strokes!"

Over at the dugout, Kip turned to Ernie and asked, "Um, what happened to practice?"

Ernie shrugged. "I think this practice is about the fence," he said.

CHAPTER FIFTEEN

Meow

The match was supposed to be a simple home game in which the Comets faced off against the Solvay Tigers.

Ernie hadn't been too concerned. The Solvay Tigers had a reputation for being a pack of total crybabies. Besides, Ernie figured, the Comets had the home park advantage—and the home park had never looked better.

Dusty had given the place a complete makeover.

"Wo-ow," Kip said to Ernie as they locked up their bikes. "I don't even recognize the old place."

"Thank you, thank you. Hold the applause," said Dusty, watching their reaction with a smug smile.

Ernie threw an arm over Dusty's shoulders. "I told you he was good," said Ernie. "I discovered him too. Did I ever tell you about that? I discovered him."

Dusty twisted until he got Ernie's arm to drop off his shoulders. It's true that Ernie had been an important figure in Dusty's career—but Dusty was getting really tired of hearing the discovery legend.

"I'll never forget it," Ernie continued. "Dusty was smashing plates and making mosaics in the wet cement of the sidewalk, and—"

Fortunately, that was the moment when Swimming Pool arrived for the game. "Dusty!" she cried from the distance as she took in the new ballpark. She started laughing and dancing all the way across the field. "I hardly recognize the place!"

"That's what I keep hearing," said Dusty. "That's a good thing, right?"

"Absolutely good!" said Swimming Pool. She threw a hammerlock on Dusty's neck. "Genius, genius, genius."

"I couldn't have done it without the whole team," said Dusty.

"I bet not," said Swimming Pool, looking over the ballpark. "And I'm glad to see you're working with the guys."

Dusty had turned the entire ballpark into a sunrise. There was a tiny crescent of the rising sun along the outfield fence at center field, half hidden in the grass, just a ridge of yellow paint. From that point, multicolored sunbeams traveled across the fence and spilled out onto the scoreboard, over the bullpens, into the bleachers, and even onto the support buildings that housed the bathrooms and the vending machines. It was a lot of yellow, of course, but some sunbeams were blue, pink, gray, and even lime green.

It was simply a remarkable sight.

Dusty was still a little concerned about one aspect of the makeover. He hadn't been able to fix the potholes in the parking lot because that took something called asphalt. All he could do was to hang a new sign that read: "Pardon Our Potholes." All the parents agreed that dodging the potholes had never been so much fun. "It used to be a drag, but now it's the Indy 500!" said Mrs. Morgenstern.

Dusty still wasn't so sure. "Do you like the pothole sign, Swimming Pool?" he asked.

"Are you kidding me?" Swimming Pool replied. "You know that pothole sign is my favorite part!" She grabbed Dusty's head for a quick rabbit haircut.

"That pothole sign is hysterical, Dusty," said Ernie.

Dusty nodded in Ernie's direction but that was all.

Dusty had saved one final touch as a surprise for the whole team. It was an official Comets pennant. All it took was cardboard and scissors to cut a stencil of a comet blazing across the sky. After that, it was basically a matter of old T-shirts and spray paint.

The surprise didn't happen until just before the game got started. Both teams usually lined the field for the national anthem. The Solvay Tigers emerged from the dugout to a nice round of applause and assembled along the first base line. No big deal.

But when the Comets emerged from the dugout, the crowd went wild. Ernie, Kip, and Swimming Pool looked over their shoulders to see what had caused the commotion. What they saw were dozens of white pennants shimmering over the bleachers. The crowd was chanting "Go, Comets! Go, Comets!" and everyone was waving a pennant, each one emblazoned with a shiny gold comet.

"Wow," said Kip, "Wow. Wow."

"You can say that again," said Swimming Pool.

"I told you," said Ernie, shaking his head. "That Dusty goes all out."

Unfortunately, after the big entrance, the game didn't go so well for the Comets. It didn't have anything to do with the fancy new colors on the ballpark. It didn't have to do with their new umpire, Mrs. Yamamoto, and her broken eyeglasses. It didn't even have anything to do with Noah Morgenstern's tendency to throw the bat.

The awful truth was that Swimming Pool was off her game.

Swimming Pool had been missing baseball practice to go to charm school but that hadn't been a problem until now. Things went wrong that had never gone wrong before. She hung a curve ball over the plate on an 0–2 count. She let go of a wild pitch that struck the Tigers' meanest player and started this whole vendetta thing. Worse than that, she walked a batter for the go-ahead run when the Tigers had the bases loaded.

The Comets dugout had started out lively but by the fourth inning, things were looking pretty grim.

"Chaos, disaster," said Kip, with his fingers and his nose pressed through the chain-link fence. "Somebody's got to talk to Swimming Pool."

134

"I know," said Ernie. "This is a disaster." He opened a piece of gum and popped it into his mouth.

When Ernie didn't budge, Kip repeated himself a little bit louder. "I said 'Chaos, disaster. Somebody's got to talk to Swimming Pool,'" said Kip. "Who could possibly be the right 'somebody' for that job?"

Everyone in the dugout was looking at Ernie.

Ernie signaled Mrs. Yamamoto for a time-out and headed for the pitcher's mound.

The bleachers grew quiet as Ernie crossed the field. One voice in the stands started chanting, "Swimming Pool, Swimming Pool!"—but nobody joined in and the chant soon died down.

Swimming Pool was wiping sweat off her forehead when Ernie arrived on the mound. "Hey, Ernie," she said.

Ernie spit into the dirt. "Hey, Pool," he said. "It's been an interesting game."

"I'll say interesting. Yes, it has," Swimming Pool replied.

"Yes, yes, yes," Ernie went on. "A lot of interesting things have been happening. Look, um, you know who's down for relief pitcher today?"

"You want to call in the relief pitcher?" said Swimming Pool. That had never happened before.

"I'm just telling you," Ernie continued. "It's Noah Morgenstern. So I would appreciate it if you told me what your problem is and how you intend to change it because I don't want to be the one who pulls you off the field and sends in Noah Morgenstern."

Swimming Pool looked into her glove. "I'm off my game. I got a lot on my mind. It's not easy being a girl."

"Not easy being a girl?" Ernie pondered this point for a moment. "Well, you're going to have to let me know how that works out for you," he said with an edge, "because I don't think I can help you with that problem." Ernie instinctively ducked in case Swimming Pool was inclined to throw a left hook. It had been known to happen.

Instead, Swimming Pool winced slightly and dropped her shoulders. "Be sensitive, Ernie," she demanded. "You could be a little more sensitive, you know?"

"Look, I'm sorry," he said. "I keep forgetting you're a girl. That must be very complicated." He looked around the mound, hoping for some kind of backup.

"What's that supposed to mean?" Swimming Pool snapped.

"I just said it's complicated, that's all," Ernie blurted defensively. "I'm an idiot with words, you know that."

Neither of them spoke for a moment. At the same time, neither left the mound. The game would wait until they got to the bottom of this situation.

"So you talk to Dusty much lately?" asked Swimming Pool.

"Not really," Ernie admitted. "He okay?"

Swimming Pool shrugged. "You see him more than I do."

"Yeah, but he talks to you," said Ernie. "He doesn't talk to me. He doesn't even like me."

"What makes you say that?"

"He ditches me," said Ernie. "He thinks I don't notice, but I do. He ditched me this morning. You were standing right there."

"I didn't notice that," said Swimming Pool.

"Well, I did," said Ernie.

They got quiet again for a moment.

"So Ernie," Swimming Pool began to say at the same time Ernie said, "So what's up with this girl problem?"

They paused again for a moment. Swimming Pool spotted Dusty at home plate who signaled the words, "You okay?" Swimming Pool nodded. Someone in the stands hollered, "Play ball!" but Ernie and Swimming Pool ignored it.

"So Ernie," Swimming Pool said, getting down to business, "you know how to dance?"

"Dance?" said Ernie. "What kind of dance?"

"Just boy-girl dance," she said. "It's not complicated."

"Well, sure," said Ernie, "I can dance. I'm not a professional, but—"

Swimming Pool was distracted by a Tiger dancing dangerously along the third base line. She fired the ball to Dusty at home plate and scared the Tiger back to third. She turned back to Ernie and said, "I want you to know this is not a date, Ernie. I just need a partner for this dance contest."

"Is this some kind of charm school thing?" said Ernie.

"Yeah, what else?" said Swimming Pool.

"So what's the difference between a dance and a dance contest?" Ernie asked.

"Silver dollars," said Swimming Pool. "Shiny silver dollars."

Ernie cooed. "I could use a few silver dollars."

"Well, here's your chance."

"This is not a date, right?" Ernie said with emphasis.

"No, it's not," Swimming Pool insisted with equal emphasis. "So does that mean you'll go?"

"Did I say yes?"

"No, you didn't. You didn't say yes or no."

"Yes, I'll go," said Ernie.

"Okay," said Swimming Pool. "Whew, that's a relief. It was either you or Noah Morgenstern." She hesitated once more to check the bases and then she said, "So listen, this conversation never happened but I'm seeing you Friday at charm school, right?"

"Right," said Ernie. "Does this take care of the girl thing or do we still have a problem?"

"Whatever," said Swimming Pool, flipping a "W" with her fingers.

As Ernie headed back to the dugout, a smattering of applause rose from the bleachers. There was some general conversation, of course, as to what Ernie and Swimming Pool had been talking about for so long on the pitcher's mound but most of that discussion was cut short when Mrs. Yamamoto hollered "Play ball!" and the next batter stepped up to the plate.

Ernie expected things to go smoothly after that—and Swimming Pool's game did improve. The Comets still limped behind the Tigers on the scoreboard—but the new sunbeam-covered scoreboard looked terrific.

There was just one more glitch in the day. But it was a biggie. Ernie was hunched in the dugout beside Swimming Pool when Ronjon stepped onto the bench and pointed into the bleachers.

"Hey, Ernie," Ronjon said, "isn't that your dad?"

Ernie followed Ronjon's finger. Sure enough, it was Red. "Sure is," Ernie said, turning back to the game.

Ronjon walked down the bench, stepping around Swimming Pool and Dusty, for a closer look into the bleachers. "And isn't that Cat Lady with him?" Swimming Pool asked.

Ernie cringed. He stiffened slightly on the bench.

"Cat Lady?" said Dusty, rising to his feet. "No way!"

Before Ernie could even look, Mrs. Yamamoto cried, "Strike three," and the Comets ran onto the field for the top of the eighth inning. When the dugout had emptied, Ernie searched the bleachers and—sure enough—there was Cat Lady sitting next to his dad.

Cat Lady happened to spot Ernie looking at them and tapped Red on the shoulder. Both of them turned toward Ernie and waved, all happy.

Ernie ducked back into the dugout. He couldn't believe it. Red never said anything about attending the ball game with anybody, much less Cat Lady.

"Hey, Ernie," said Kip. "Call me crazy but isn't that—?"

"You're crazy," said Ernie, stepping out of the dugout.

"But I didn't even finish my sentence!" said Kip.

He followed Ernie onto the third base line to watch the inning get under way. The first thing Ernie noticed, however, was how quickly the story about his dad and Cat Lady was traveling across the ballfield.

"Hey, Marcus!" cried Ronjon from shortstop.

"Hey, what?" cried Marcus.

"Isn't that Cat Lady with Ernie's dad?"

"Where?"

"Hey, Larry!" cried Chuck in the outfield.

"Check it out!" cried Larry.

"What?" cried Noah Morgenstern.

"Heads up, you guys," barked Ernie. "Keep your eye on the game!" But it was too late for that. Word about his dad and Cat Lady had spread like wildfire.

"Ernie, hey Ernie!" Marcus hollered, with his hands cupped to his face.

"Hey, what?" said Ernie.

"Meow!" cried Marcus.

Laughter surged across the field. Ernie cringed and held his breath, hoping the "Meow" gag wouldn't catch on.

"Hey, Ernie!" cried Ronjon. "Meow!"

And then Chuck. And then Larry. Even Noah Morgenstern. It didn't take long before the whole team was meowing from the field. Sick cats, hungry cats, cuddly cats, fighting cats.

Of course, the people in the bleachers figured it was some funny joke about the Solvay Tigers.

But Swimming Pool knew what was going on. She threw a sympathetic look at Ernie but by this point he had already thrown up a steely defense. He was studying the scoreboard with concern, seemingly unaffected by the catcalls.

But Swimming Pool knew different. She turned toward the outfield, raised both arms and shook the ball. She was ready to pitch if the team was ready to play.

Ernie relaxed a bit once Swimming Pool got the game going. He couldn't relax completely because he was fairly sure the ribbing would last for some time. He absolutely knew he hadn't heard his last meow.

"I don't get it," said Kip. "What was that about? What's the joke? 'Meow'?"

CHAPTER SIXTEEN

Victory Lap

Ernie was on time for charm school. Swimming Pool was late. "Gee, what else is new?" thought Ernie.

He expected to see more boys in the lobby of Miss Ginger's School of Tap & Tumbling but so far he was the only one. For some reason, that made him the object of much whispering and giggling. Ernie thought that he had dressed okay for the event. He was wearing his good pants, his good shoes, and his good sweater. It was the same outfit he wore whenever his dad made him go to church. But, apparently, the girls thought Ernie looked funny. Or something.

Ernie didn't get it. Girls didn't giggle or whisper about him at school. He wasn't entirely sure what was going on. All he knew was that he felt completely out of his element—which more or less seemed to be happening all the time these days.

Ernie was enormously relieved when he heard another boy's voice say, "Ernie Castellano, of all people!" He was doubly relieved when he turned to find Tony.

"Tony!" cried Ernie. "I haven't seen you since that day at the Moose Lodge!"

They shook hands and laughed and gave each other a slap on the back like they were lifelong friends—which, in a way, they were.

Tony had really dressed for the event. He was wearing a dark sports coat that looked as if it might have been a hand-me-down. It looked as if Tony would grow into the sleeves next year. He also wore an emerald green necktie that was so long he had to tuck it into his trousers. Even so, one loose end of necktie slipped back up to peek over his belt loops. The tie was held fast to his shirt with a small tie clasp emblazoned with the word TONY.

"Nice tie," Ernie offered.

"Yeah," muttered Tony. "My mom says it brings out my eyes."

"You here for charm school?" Ernie asked.

"Not here for a flu shot," said Tony. He checked his profile in a hall mirror, ran a comb through his hair, wiped the comb against his thigh, and tucked it in his hip pocket.

"Well, I gotta say," Ernie continued, "I think that's great, you being in charm school. I know plenty of guys who could learn from your example. It's courageous, really. In fact, ever since Swimming Pool signed up, I've been thinking I could use a little charm school myself. Learn how to, you know, open doors and hold chairs and—"

Ernie hesitated because Tony was staring at him blankly.

Tony blinked twice as if he couldn't believe his ears. He looked Ernie square in the face. "Castellano," he said bluntly, "I'm only here because I'm getting *paid*."

"Huh?" Ernie was dumbfounded. "What?"

"Betty hired me," Tony explained.

"Oh," said Ernie. "I thought you were here for charm school."

"Yeah, well, I'm good for the dance contest." Tony gave his necktie a tug. "I'm surprised at you, Ernie," he said with a smile. "I don't need charm school. I am oozing with charm."

At that moment, Miss Ginger opened the studio door with a breezy "Hello!" All the children surged forward to file into the adjoining room for charm school. Ernie was suddenly caught up in the tide of kids swept toward the door. He looked around, desperately seeking Swimming Pool in the crowd, and that's when, naturally, Swimming Pool came barreling through the front door, a little sweaty and out of breath.

"Ernie!" Swimming Pool cried. "Whew! Glad I made it. What are you waiting for? Let's go inside!"

As it turned out, none of the boys from Miss Ginger's tumbling, modeling, or karate classes bothered to accept Miss Ginger's invitation to attend her dance contest. Swimming Pool was not alone among the girls who found this piece of information slightly disconcerting but since Swimming Pool had Ernie in tow, she tried to be magnanimous for the girls who were stuck dancing with other girls.

There were only two boys in the room besides Ernie. One was Tony who had, of course, been hired by Betty for the occasion. The second was none other than Noah Morgenstern. Noah accompanied his sister Amanda Morgenstern and accosted Ernie with a cup of punch in each fist and a mouthful of cookies. "Hey, Ernie!" Noah yammered. "Fancy party, huh?"

Ernie nodded and smiled—but as he turned away, he shot Swimming Pool a look. "Oh, great," he muttered. "Noah Morgenstern. My new best friend."

Betty was making a big deal of finding the right table to sit at with Tony. In the scramble for seats, Swimming Pool managed to tug on Gina's sleeve and ask, "Hey, Gina, what gives? I thought you said you were going to invite your brother."

"I was," said Gina, "until my brother reminded me he'd rather be dead." Swimming Pool laughed. She knew what brothers were like. She flipped Gina an underhanded double-okay sign that was Dusty's code for "Oh, I gotcha."

Miss Ginger started walking purposefully around the room the way she did when she wanted everyone's full attention. She was parading around in a big, pink, flouncy hat with a wide brim and ribbons.

"What's up with the hat?" asked Gina.

"Dunno," said Swimming Pool. "What's up with the hat?"

"Don't look at me," said Ernie. "I'm not from this planet."

"Welcome, welcome, welcome!" Miss Ginger chimed. She pumped up the enthusiasm for the sake of the three boys in the room. "Today is rather an exciting day because we are holding the big dance contest!" she announced. Miss Ginger

paused for applause. When none came, she quickly continued, "Let me review the rules."

Miss Ginger reached into one of her gloves and
removed a small note card on which the official rules were
encoded. "This dance contest," she declared, "is a little bit
complicated. When the music stops, the dancers freeze—and
if you are doing the dance that I call out from three random
cards, you will be asked to leave the floor."

"Hunh?" the group cried out as one. "What?" No one
seemed to understand Miss Ginger's explanation at all.

Swimming Pool leaned toward Ernie as Miss Ginger
launched into her explanation again. "It's like freeze tag," said
Swimming Pool, "only the loser is doing the wrong dance at
the wrong time. She's going to stop the music, call out a
dance, and all the people doing that dance have to leave the
floor."

"Got it," said Ernie. "You done this before?"

"Something like it at camp," Swimming Pool said.

Miss Ginger was full of tricks today. She reached into
her other glove to reveal the three random cards. Each card
contained the name of a dance. She held up the first card and
read: "Cowboy."

There was a titter of recognition from the girls. They
wiggled in their seats with excitement. The Cowboy Dance
was a big favorite.

"What's the Cowboy?" said Ernie.

"You twirl a lasso," said Swimming Pool. "Ride a pony.
No big deal."

Miss Ginger held up the second card and announced,
"Monkey!"

There was a bigger titter of recognition from the girls. Ernie looked lost, so Swimming Pool leaned over to explain. "The monkey is a dance from the old days," she said. "You jerk like a monkey."

Ernie looked blank. "I don't even know what that means," he said.

"Lastly," Miss Ginger announced, displaying the final card, "The Box Step!"

All the girls gasped. The Box Step had consumed one entire unnerving day of charm school. The Box Step was quite nearly impossible to do without making a mistake. Many girls that day had gone home in tears.

Swimming Pool was silent for a moment. She hadn't expected Miss Ginger to spring anything quite so technical as the Box Step. When she hadn't offered the usual explanation, Ernie leaned over to say, "Okay, I give. What's with the Box?"

She paused before answering. "You know how geometry looks easy but it's hard?" she said. "That's the Box. It takes a little coordination."

Ernie gasped slightly. He didn't mean to gasp but Swimming Pool thought she heard one. "Coordination? Um, Swimming Pool," Ernie continued, like nothing whatsoever was wrong, "um, you know how I said I could dance?"

Miss Ginger was shaking a small velvet pouch with a jingle and a jangle. "And in case I need to remind anyone," she said dramatically.

"Silver dollars!" the children cried. The room went crazy.

Swimming Pool looked at Ernie. "Right, you said you could dance. You can dance, right? Right?"

"Well, sure I can dance," Ernie said, "but I'm not so good at the coordination thing. Like, I can do the polka dance."

"What's the polka dance?" asked Swimming Pool.

"It's when your aunt grabs you and you just hold on," Ernie explained.

Swimming Pool wasn't quite sure what to say. She stammered, blustered, and fumed a bit. "Well, we didn't learn the polka dance in charm school. We learned the Box."

"So teach me," said Ernie.

"I can't teach you now!" said Swimming Pool, gesturing frantically at the room. "The dance contest is about to begin!"

Miss Ginger had removed her big pink hat. She placed the dance cards inside and was stirring them to add to the excitement. "Round and round they go!" she said in that singsong way, "and where they stop, nobody oh!" Miss Ginger interrupted herself and raised one finger aloft to make one last additional point. "If there should be a tie—," she began to announce.

"Look, okay, let's not worry about it," said Ernie. "You heard the rules. This is not a dance 'competition.' It's a game of chance. We have to do the right dance at the right time—but we don't have to do it well."

"Unless there's a tie-breaker," said Swimming Pool. "If there's a tie-breaker, the winner is the one who does the best dance!"

"When did she say that?" asked Ernie.

"Just now while you were talking!" snapped Swimming Pool.

"Well—we can't worry about that now!" said Ernie.

"I told Miss Ginger this was ridiculous," Swimming Pool groused, collapsing in her chair. "I told her boys don't dance."

"Um, I wouldn't bank on that," said Ernie. He shot his eyes at Tony. Betty was whispering to Tony with as much enthusiasm as Swimming Pool had been whispering to him, although Tony didn't appear to be listening. He was more preoccupied with his comb.

"You know Tony?" said Ernie. "Tony can dance. I saw him dancing with a waxer once. He's really good."

"Dancing with a waxer?" Swimming Pool asked.

"Long story. Trust me. The boy cuts a rug."

"Figures," Swimming Pool said with a huff. "You know Betty paid him to be here."

Ernie wasn't shocked by the news, of course, but he was surprised to hear Swimming Pool say it. "How do you know that?"

Swimming Pool rolled her eyes. "It's a room full of girls, Ernie. Word gets around. Everybody knows everything. There are no secrets here. Girls are like that."

Ernie nodded, scoffed, and screwed up his lips. "Yeah, well let me tell you something," he said. "Boys are like that too."

Swimming Pool arched an eyebrow. She figured Ernie was talking about the day at the ballpark when the team made the joke about Cat Lady with all the cats in the field but she thought it was only polite to play dumb. She looked at Ernie as if she didn't understand what he meant. "Boys too?" said Swimming Pool.

"Don't play that," said Ernie. "You heard. I know you heard."

"Heard about what?" she asked, even though she knew she wouldn't be able to play dumb much longer.

Ernie leaned in close so that he didn't have to say it too loud. "About Dad and Cat Lady," he said.

Swimming Pool couldn't suppress a slight smile. She understood how the news might seem bad to Ernie but it wasn't really so bad at all. "I hate to tell you this, Ernie," she said, "but they make a nice couple."

Ernie studied Swimming Pool to make sure she wasn't lying. "You really think so?"

"Yeah," said Swimming Pool. "They fit."

It was the sudden screech of music that made them jump out of their chairs. Miss Ginger had gone ahead and started the boom box without telling them to get onto the dance floor. Swimming Pool grabbed Ernie's arm and dragged him as she pushed through all the other children who were already crowding the space.

"Okay," said Ernie. "Now I'm nervous. My palms are sweating."

"Here," said Swimming Pool. "Wipe them off on my gloves."

"Good idea," said Ernie. "I was wondering what those gloves were for." Ernie and Swimming Pool grabbed hands and shook them vigorously as they faced off on the dance floor. "Better?" Swimming Pool asked, even as they shook. Ernie nodded and they dropped hands.

"Okay," said Swimming Pool, "pick a dance."

Ernie went with his gut. "Monkey," he said.

Ernie and Swimming Pool managed to sail through the first elimination by gyrating like a couple of monkeys. Ernie felt stupid at first but then Swimming Pool said, "Look around." After Ernie caught sight of Noah Morgenstern doing the Cowboy, he felt a lot better. Suddenly he felt like Fred Astaire.

That was when Miss Ginger stopped the music. All the kids waited with bated breath. She drew a card from her hat and announced, "Cowboy."

Ernie and Swimming Pool cried, "Yes!" They slapped high-five and held their ground as the cowboys left the floor. "Okay, what next?" Swimming Pool said, elbowing Ernie.

"Maybe . . . Cowboy?" Ernie suggested. "It's not likely to come up twice in a row."

"Saddle up, pardner," said Swimming Pool. She showed Ernie how to twirl a lasso and ride a pony by rocking on his heels. Ernie caught on soon enough.

Just as abruptly as before, Miss Ginger stopped the music. She drew another card and announced, "Monkey!"

Ernie and Swimming Pool jumped up and down a few times and clapped their hands. They couldn't contain their excitement. The adrenalin was contagious. They nervously stepped aside so that all the monkeys could leave the dance floor. And a considerable pack of monkeys had been picked off in that round.

Miss Ginger didn't want disappointment to dispel the excitement of the dance contest so she took the time to shake the velvet bag and cry, "What's that sound?" The sad monkeys groaned, "Silver dollars!" as they returned to their chairs.

"Okay, what next?" asked Ernie.

Swimming Pool grimaced. "My guess? The Box Step."

"Not the Box Step," said Ernie, shaking his head. "That's too obvious."

Swimming Pool balked. "Ernie, sooner or later, you gotta do the Box Step!"

"But not now! Trust me! I'm good with numbers!"

Swimming Pool stamped her foot. "So what then?"

Ernie fretted as he said, "Cowboy?"

Swimming Pool rolled her eyes. "I'm sick of doing the Cowboy!"

"Trust me," said Ernie, "Cowboy." He had already hitched up and was riding off into the sunset. The music hadn't even started yet. Swimming Pool issued a little grunt of annoyance, grabbed her lasso, and saddled up behind.

In this round, the music stopped almost as soon as it had started. Everybody held their breath. Miss Ginger looked at the card in her hand and said:

"Box Step."

Swimming Pool and Ernie jumped and screamed and jumped and screamed and jumped and screamed. When they finally stopped jumping and screaming because they had to catch their breath, they looked across the floor to see that there was only one other couple remaining.

It was Betty and Tony.

"Oh, no," said Swimming Pool. "A tie-breaker!" When she looked at Ernie, they both had the same expression: Slack-jawed and wide-eyed.

"Okay!" said Miss Ginger, brimming with excitement.

"Here we go! This decides it! I am about to reach into my hat and draw the name of a dance. The couple that does the best job dancing that dance is the winner of the dance contest!" She held out the hat and poised one gloved hand above it.

"Um, excuse me?" a voice called out.

Miss Ginger hesitated and looked onto the dance floor.

It was Tony. With a toothy smile, he signaled Miss Ginger for a brief time-out and dropped to one knee to tighten his shoelaces.

Betty took the moment to look at Swimming Pool. She smiled and sighed as though it was all over except for those silver dollars. "Well, Swimming Pool," said Betty, "this should be interesting."

Swimming Pool and Ernie smiled back but neither of them could think of anything to say.

Once Tony had double-knotted both his shoes, he rose to his feet and nodded at Miss Ginger to go ahead and draw that little dance card.

Nobody noticed—not Tony, not Swimming Pool, not Ernie, not Betty—not even Miss Ginger—but as Tony stood up, his comb slipped out of his pocket and fell to the floor.

Miss Ginger looked at the card in her hand and announced "Box Step."

The room gasped. And the music began to play.

Swimming Pool was stuck between shock and panic. But Ernie stepped toward her and spread his arms wide. "Okay, Pool," he said, "This is it. Teach me the Box."

"Well, it's like one foot here and one foot there," Swimming Pool began.

"Don't explain it to me," said Ernie, "we don't have time. Just start doing the dance and I'll keep up. Trust me. My aunt does this to me all the time."

"Okay, well," Swimming Pool continued, "it's just a box."

Swimming Pool started measuring the steps but Ernie stood still. He had glanced over at Betty and Tony. Tony was having a tougher time with Betty than he had with the waxer at the Moose Lodge but he still looked pretty good on the old dance floor.

"Pay attention, Ernie," said Swimming Pool with an edge. "You step around the four corners of a box. It's like, it's like—"

That was when Swimming Pool had an excellent idea. Her eyes got a little wide as the notion occurred to her. Ernie noticed the change in her face and said, "What? What's up? What's the matter?"

"Watch my face," said Swimming Pool, taking charge. "The girl has the tougher part because I have to do this backward. But just take a deep breath and follow me." She gripped his hand tightly and stood a little straighter. "We're just going to walk around the bases," she said.

"Walk around the bases?" said Ernie.

"Like baseball. It's like hitting the ball over the fence and getting to walk a home run," said Swimming Pool. "Step to first base," she said, tugging Ernie toward her. Ernie took one step forward while Swimming Pool took one step behind. "That's good," Swimming Pool continued, "then second base, hold up." Ernie took one step to the side with Swimming Pool and then brought both feet together as he waited for further instruction.

"Okay, third base," Swimming Pool continued. She stepped forward, pushing Ernie backward to finish off the square. "And home."

"That's it?" said Ernie, surprised at how smoothly the Box had gone.

"Yeah, except we have to do it over and over and over," said Swimming Pool.

"You lead," said Ernie. "I'll follow."

"Actually it's the other way around, but never mind about that now," said Swimming Pool, as they started another box.

It wasn't the most perfect Box Step in the world. Ernie stepped on Swimming Pool's toes more than once. A couple of times, Swimming Pool lost track between second base and third and had to start over from a new home plate. They weren't exactly stepping to the beat and Ernie kept forgetting not to look down. However, as Box Steps go, this was definitely a box. It totally deserved a passing grade.

Unfortunately, it still couldn't compete with Tony on the dance floor. True to form, Tony was oozing confidence as he and Betty glided through one box after another. Betty looked slightly stunned but kept a game smile. Tony was almost working the crowd as he and Betty circled the floor. Ernie and Swimming Pool were mostly sort of stuck in the middle.

And then it happened. Tony tried to get Betty to do that

under-the-arm maneuver he'd been practicing with the waxer. Betty survived the first half of the step but when Tony went to pivot on one foot so that he was facing Betty again, his foot landed right on his own comb.

Tony never knew what hit him. His shoe skidded out from underneath and the next thing anybody knew was that Tony was falling. He gripped Betty's hand for support and suddenly she was falling too. Betty cried, "No-o-o" as she was heading down for the count and it was a long time before that single word came up for air.

At first, Ernie and Swimming Pool were too busy clocking off the bases to notice what had happened. But when they heard a gasp rise from the crowd, they looked over to see Tony and Betty sprawled on the floor. After that, they saw Miss Ginger with her mouth open.

"I think we won," said Swimming Pool, hardly believing it was possible. They kept the Box Step going as they looked over the crowd.

"We're the only ones dancing," said Ernie. "I think you're right. I think we won."

"We won, we won!" Swimming Pool screamed. She broke hands with Ernie, ran to Miss Ginger, and snatched the velvet bag from her hand. Then Swimming Pool raised both arms overhead and burst into a victory lap around the dance floor. "We won, we won, we won!" she cried.

Unfortunately, as Swimming Pool was completing her victory lap, she ran smack into Miss Ginger. "I'm afraid not!" said Miss Ginger, grabbing the velvet bag out of Swimming Pool's hand. "The judges have not yet determined the tie-breaker!"

She gestured at three chairs positioned on the far edge of the dance floor. Seated in those chairs were Finny, Fanny, and Noah Morgenstern.

"When did they become the judges?" said Ernie.

"Back when you were talking!" groused Swimming Pool.

"Let's hear from the judges," said Miss Ginger, in an even tone. Finny, Fanny and Noah conferred among themselves and then pointed across the floor to where Tony and Betty were sprawled on the ground.

"I can't believe it!" Betty cried, bursting into tears. "I simply can't believe it!"

"I can't believe it either," muttered Swimming Pool.

The crowd broke into applause as Tony helped Betty to her feet. As Miss Ginger presented them with their silver dollars, the other kids pressed in with congratulations. Ernie looked at Swimming Pool and shrugged. "Win a few, lose a few," he said.

Swimming Pool and Ernie headed over to congratulate the winners—but Miss Ginger dropped a hand on Swimming Pool's shoulder and pulled her aside. Ernie stopped as well but Miss Ginger gestured that he wasn't needed. "I need a word alone with Swimming Pool, young man," said Miss Ginger.

"Yes, ma'am," said Ernie, throwing a last glance at Swimming Pool as though she was being hauled off to the principal's office.

Miss Ginger led Swimming Pool into her cramped little office. Swimming Pool noticed that Miss Ginger still hadn't cleaned the place up although, as Swimming Pool admitted to herself, "I'm not one to talk."

"Swimming Pool, that was the most uncouth display I have ever seen," said Miss Ginger.

"I thought I'd won," said Swimming Pool. "I was excited!"

"Even winners need to be gracious," said Miss Ginger. She acted as though the words were hard to find—which was usual, coming from Miss Ginger. "I'm afraid your outburst today has put me quite completely over the edge." Miss Ginger sounded almost overcome with emotion. She couldn't even look Swimming Pool in the eye.

"You don't mean?" Swimming Pool uttered, feeling herself well up with tears.

"You're overexcited, Swimming Pool," said Miss Ginger, suddenly dismissive. "I'll let you return to your friend. But I need to speak with your mother when she picks you up after charm school today."

With that, Miss Ginger left the office to return to the studio. Swimming Pool sighed and dropped her head. She noticed a long pink ribbon on the floor and picked it up. Her hands were shaking slightly. She needed something to do with her hands.

"What's the matter?" said Ernie, when Swimming Pool returned from her powwow with Miss Ginger. Swimming Pool looked flushed and pale but he didn't think she'd been crying. It wasn't like Swimming Pool to cry. Certainly not about anything so stupid as charm school.

Swimming Pool didn't answer. She was wrapping a pink

ribbon about one hand, and then unwrapping it in the other direction. She seemed really distracted.

"So what's up?" Ernie continued. "What'd she say? What happened?"

"I'm sunk," said Swimming Pool. "It's over. Finito. Kaput."

CHAPTER SEVENTEEN

Like, But Not Like

"I don't hate you, Betty," said Swimming Pool.

"Are you sure?" asked Betty, with genuine need. "I think if you're really honest with yourself, you must hate me a little."

"Well, no, I don't," said Swimming Pool, "so get over it already."

Swimming Pool had been partnered with Betty for computer class so they had to share the same desk and the same monitor. Some days Betty wasn't so bad. Other days Betty refused to shut up and Swimming Pool couldn't get anything done. "Computers aren't that difficult," Swimming Pool had said to Gina, "but Betty sure is."

"I mean," Betty continued, "I saw how much you wanted to win that dance contest and if I wanted to win the contest as much as you wanted to win the contest and I had been beaten by me—"

"I don't hate you, Betty," said Swimming Pool, "so drop it before I do."

Betty was quiet for a moment. "Okay," she said, seeming satisfied. "But does Ernie hate me?"

"How should I know? Ask Ernie."

"I figured you'd know," said Betty. "You talk to him all the time."

"I do not talk to him all the time."

"That's not what I heard," said Betty. "I heard you pass him notes and everything."

"I have no idea what you're talking about," said Swimming Pool. "Is this computer class or is this Spanish? Because you and I are not talking the same language." Swimming Pool returned to the monitor and hit Enter. The assignment was to search the Web for instructions on how to build a birdcage and so far they weren't having any luck.

"Kirsten said she saw you in the library," Betty continued. "One time, long time ago, like weeks."

Kirsten had been in the library when Swimming Pool handed Ernie her list of all the things she didn't like.

"Nothing pink, nothing goofy," Kirsten told Betty. "It was like, if you're going to buy me a present, this is all the stuff I don't like." That was Kirsten's analysis.

Betty and Kirsten had looked at each other, wide-eyed with alarm. "How long has this been going on?" Betty asked.

"Who knows?" said Kirsten. "But doesn't it make sense?"

Swimming Pool was peering intently at the computer screen like it was the first time she'd seen a search engine. Unfortunately, her search had yet to bring up anything about birdcages.

"Kirsten said it was a list," said Betty, not letting the subject drop. "Something about 'Nothing pink, nothing goofy.'"

"I have no idea what you're talking about," Swimming Pool said, although, of course she remembered that day in the library. But what did Betty need to know about that? Or Kirsten for that matter? "Can we get back to the computer, please?"

"Oh, Swimming Pool," said Betty. "I can do computers in my sleep." She seized the keyboard, typed in new search words concerning the birdcage, hit Enter, and let the computer do its thing. The search results soon began to spill across the screen.

"You're good," said Swimming Pool. She hated to admit it, but Betty was really good.

Betty thought she'd take Swimming Pool off the hook for a while. But then she couldn't resist.

"Swimming Pool," she ventured, "if somebody liked you, would you want to know?"

"Betty," Swimming Pool groaned irritably.

Betty was convinced that Swimming Pool was just being difficult. Swimming Pool was just playing dumb. So Betty hit the nail on the head. "I know who likes you," she said.

"What are you talking about now?" said Swimming Pool.

"I know who likes you," Betty repeated. "And it's a boy." Betty said the word *boy* like it was served up with fudge sauce, two cherries, and a swirl of whipped cream.

"Betty, you are too much," said Swimming Pool.

"Okay," said Betty dismissively. "If you don't care to know, I'm not going to tell you. But the whole school's talking."

"Talking about what?"

"About who likes you," said Betty.

Somehow Swimming Pool felt vaguely threatened.

"I think you know," Betty continued.

"I think I don't," said Pool.

"I think you do," Betty urged.

"I really don't want to play this game," snapped Swimming Pool.

Betty groaned dramatically. "Oh, come on, Swimming Pool! Who doesn't want to know who likes them?"

Swimming Pool tapped the mouse irritably. Of course, on some level, Swimming Pool was dying of curiosity. But her instincts told her that she was headed for a trap.

"Okay, I'll tell you," said Betty. She was obviously busting with the news.

"No!" cried Swimming Pool. "If somebody likes me, I don't want to know."

"I think you do," said Betty in the same singsong cadence they used at charm school. "I think you know. I think you already know."

Swimming Pool felt like she was never going to get out of this conversation alive. "Okay," she said, "I give. You wore me down. Who likes me? I want to know."

Betty pursed her lips at Swimming Pool. The gig was up. "Swimming Pool," she said, "you surprise me. You mean to tell me that you don't know already?"

"Betty, if you don't stop playing with me, I am going to explode."

Betty opened her palms as if she had nothing to hide. "Ernie," she said, letting the cat out of the bag. "It's Ernie. There, I said it. Ernie, Ernie, Ernie."

Swimming Pool balked. "What are you talking about? Ernie? Castellano? He's my friend!"

"Exactly," said Betty. "He's your friend. He's a boy. He's your boyfriend." To Betty, this kind of reasoning made more sense than a computer.

"This is ridiculous," cried Swimming Pool. "I like him as a friend but I don't like him the way you mean I like him."

"There," Betty said, triumphantly, "you admitted it."

"I didn't admit anything," Swimming Pool protested.

"You just said you liked him," Betty insisted. "You just said it about three times."

Swimming Pool was starting to blow her top. "Like but not like," she said, punching every word like she was hammering a nail. "I mean I only like him as a friend."

Betty smiled sweetly and dropped her shoulders. "Swimming Pool," she said with mild reproach, "you don't have to pretend for me. I know about the note."

"That wasn't a note!" Swimming Pool protested. "That was just a list I wrote in the library. It had to do with—never mind what it had to do with." Swimming Pool was blustering now.

"Not that note," said Betty. "I'm talking about the other note."

"The other note? What note is that?" said Swimming Pool.

"The note in glitter," answered Betty.

There was a rumor running through school about the note in glitter.

Ronjon had heard from someone on good authority that Ernie had found a note in his backpack that was written in glitter. Glitter had been used in art class that year and it had been such a disaster that Mr. Hamilton, the art teacher, swore "Never again." If somebody was writing notes in glitter, they were going to a lot of trouble. Glitter was hard to work with—and it wasn't easy to find.

Nobody knew for sure what had actually been written on the note in glitter but speculation ran wild. Some kids thought it was the kind of poem found on valentines. Something that rhymed "true" or "blue" with "you." Other kids thought it was probably something like the motto on a sweetheart candy. "Be mine" or "Hey, cutie!"

"Something short and to the point," said Gina to Kirsten at the cafeteria table, "because it can't be easy to write in glitter." Kirsten agreed.

Of course, nobody had the nerve to ask Ernie anything about the note in glitter. And for his part, Ernie hadn't mentioned the note in glitter to anyone since the day he found it. Ronjon wouldn't say who told him about the note in glitter but he swore he had it on good authority and he swore it wasn't Ernie. So who mentioned the note to Ronjon in the first place?

Swimming Pool caught up with Dusty at a cafeteria table. "So Dusty," she said, "what do you know about this note in glitter?"

Dusty was drinking milk at the time. It almost came out his nose. "I don't know anything about a note in glitter," Dusty protested.

"I didn't say you wrote it," Swimming Pool shot back, even though Dusty owned more glitter than any kid she knew. "I just want to know what you know about it."

"All I know," said Dusty, "is that kids say Ernie found a note in glitter in his backpack. And nobody knows what it says."

"It's not about me, is it?" Swimming Pool asked.

"How should I know?" said Dusty. "Is it?"

"How should I know?" cried Swimming Pool. "Has anybody asked Ernie?"

Dusty shrugged. "Ernie doesn't talk to me anymore," he said. "Of course, it's not like I see much of you anymore either."

"That's not true," said Swimming Pool.

"Think about it, Swimming Pool," said Dusty. "The only time we talk, you're on the pitcher's mound and I'm behind home plate and we're talking in signs." Dusty held up the sign for "You know it's true."

Swimming Pool didn't argue. She considered Dusty from the other side of the cafeteria table. If she was really honest with herself, she had to admit that Dusty had in fact grown since the last time they'd had a good talk. His hair was longer, he'd put on weight, he was a little taller.

For a moment, Swimming Pool almost felt guilty—except that kids grew so quickly at Dusty's age that she could hardly hold herself to blame. "You know I been busy, right?" she asked.

"Right," said Dusty. "Busy with Ernie on the pitcher's mound. And busy with Ernie at charm school."

"What is that supposed to mean?"

"Only that it's no big surprise if people are talking," said Dusty.

Swimming Pool didn't run into Ernie at school so she made a point of stopping by the ballpark during practice.

Naturally, the Comets got really excited at the sight of Swimming Pool storming onto the ballfield—but she didn't grab a glove and she didn't grab a ball. The only thing that Swimming Pool grabbed was Ernie's collar. She dragged him toward the dugout.

"What's the big deal?" Ernie protested.

"You tell me," said Swimming Pool. "What's the deal with this note in glitter?"

"What note in glitter?"

"That's what I want to know," Swimming Pool insisted. "People say you have a note in glitter and people say I wrote it."

"Well, did you?" Ernie asked.

"No!"

"Then it's none of your business," said Ernie.

"It's my business if people are talking about me," argued Swimming Pool.

"Since when did you care what people say?"

"I don't!" said Swimming Pool. "But even Dusty says people are talking. You know it's gone out of control when even Dusty says that people are talking."

"Dusty," thought Ernie. He threw a glance at home plate. Dusty was the only one who had ever glimpsed the note in glitter. "Dusty needs to learn to keep his mouth shut," Ernie snapped.

"Leave Dusty out of this," said Swimming Pool.

"Leave me out of it!" Ernie bellowed. "All I did was open my knapsack! I didn't put the note in there!"

"Well I didn't either," said Swimming Pool.

"I never said you did!"

After that, the conversation degenerated into a rapid volley of "You shaddup," "No, you shaddup." Dusty leaned against the chain-link fence at home plate and kept his catcher's mask firmly in position. "This is all my fault," he said to himself—but it was already out of his hands. There was nothing he could do about it.

By this point, the rest of the Comets had abandoned their positions and were watching the shouting match like it was a ping-pong game. The "shaddups" were volleying back and forth with considerable fury.

All the Comets were convinced. In fact, there was very little dissent. Whatever people were saying about Swimming Pool and Ernie, it was probably true.

CHAPTER EIGHTEEN

The Rules of Fred

Swimming Pool's fifth-grade class did not have an ordinary hall pass.

The year before, Mrs. Ahearn, the fifth-grade teacher, had used a long block of wood marked "HALL PASS" in big black letters. Unfortunately, kids were always leaving it behind in the lavatory or wherever. Mrs. Ahearn gave countless lectures on accountability but the lectures never seemed to help that block of wood.

This year, Mrs. Ahearn had a new plan. She returned from a summer vacation in Maine with a big red plastic lobster. On the first day of school, she said, "This is Fred" and held the lobster aloft. "Fred is our hall pass."

The kids looked at each other as though Mrs. Ahearn had lost her mind in Maine. But Mrs. Ahearn was delighted with herself. She placed Fred in an empty fish tank by the door and added enough water to fill the tank. "Fred lives in salt water, not fresh," she explained, adding a healthy dose of table salt. "If this was fresh water, Fred would drown." The kids shuddered at the thought of Fred drowning but then they remembered that Fred wasn't real. He was plastic.

At first it was strange, but soon the kids were totally into Fred. After Mrs. Ahearn decided that the Student of the Week got to change the salt water in Fred's tank, kids clamored for the title. When Swimming Pool was Student of the Week, she tried to explain the big deal to her parents, but she gave up when they got stuck on the difference between a real lobster and a fake one.

As it was, Principal Bridwell would finish the Pledge of Allegiance over the P.A. system every morning. Then Mrs. Ahearn would instruct the fifth grade to turn from the flag toward the tank to deliver the Pledge to Fred. The Pledge to Fred went something like this:

> I know that he's plastic,
> I know that he's red.
> Still I obey the Rules of Fred.

The Rules of Fred meant that students had to use the lobster instead of a hall pass. Whenever students had to leave the classroom, they had to reach into the water, grab Fred, and take the lobster along. When students returned to the classroom, they had to plunk Fred back into the water. Simple as that.

Mrs. Ahearn was mighty pleased with herself because

the Rules of Fred worked so well for a while. A kid couldn't misplace Fred. He went in his tank by the door. It was unthinkable to forget Fred in the lavatory or the dean's office or wherever. Fred belonged back in the classroom in his tank. He couldn't be away from water for long.

Unfortunately, as early as October, the Rules of Fred began to break down. It wasn't the kids. The kids had nothing to do with it. The problem was that Fred started taking little field trips all by himself.

Fred was in the cafeteria on Seafood Friday with his claws stuck in the coleslaw and pickles. The whole school knew about Fred after that little stunt. A week later, Fred was in the library, lying on top of the dictionary with a pair of eyeglasses as if he were actually reading the definition of *crustacean*.

Sometimes, Fred got into trouble even when it wasn't his fault. During student elections, half the posters in the halls read: "Vote for Fred!" Mrs. Ahearn threatened to expel Fred from the classroom. "But Fred didn't do it!" Ronjon argued. "Fred can't write!" He held up the lobster and wiggled its claw. "Fred can't even hold a pen!" Swimming Pool added.

Fred's most notorious adventure occurred at a flagpole assembly. It wasn't an official holiday—because they didn't get the day off—but it was one of those days when the entire school had to gather on the blacktop in the hot sun while the Safety Patrol formed a big circle around the flagpole. Mr. Bridwell made a speech about patriotism. The school band performed a courageous and somewhat noisy rendition of "Stars and Stripes Forever." After that, the Safety

Patrol hooked the flag to the flagpole and yanked on the rope.

Up went the flag—and up went Fred.

Mrs. Ahearn was decidedly not amused. She gave another huge lecture on accountability but the class argued that Fred didn't understand. "Fred can't listen!" said Ronjon, shaking the lobster and flinging drops of water.

"Fred doesn't even have ears!" Swimming Pool added.

Mrs. Ahearn was all prepared to expel Fred from the classroom but for some reason she couldn't bring herself to reach into the tank and do it. It was easier, she decided, to let the plastic lobster "lie there and rot!"

But Fred didn't seem to have any intention of lying around his tank. "No doubt about it," Swimming Pool said, "that Fred is frisky." These days, it was not unlikely for Mrs. Ahearn to start any given school day with an exasperated, "Okay, has anybody seen Fred?"

Swimming Pool's hands were soaking wet because Fred was asleep in his tank that morning when she asked permission to use the lavatory. Swimming Pool whistled down the hallway, elbowed her way into the girls' room, and propped Fred on the windowsill so he could enjoy the view and not disturb the other girls. After Swimming Pool washed her hands, she grabbed Fred off the ledge, tucked him under her arm, and walked back into the hall.

Swimming Pool decided to take the long loop back to class so that she could stop by the good water fountain. For some reason, the fifth-grade classroom was stuck by the bad water fountain where the water was chalky and warm. The band room was next to the good water fountain where the water was always crystal clear and ice-cold. Swimming Pool was convinced that the location of the good water fountain was one of the most important things she had learned in three years at Pembrook Middle School.

She leaned over the fountain for a healthy slurp. Then, feeling generous, she held the knob while Fred took a slurp. Third period must have been the music hour because the band was rehearsing something next door. Swimming Pool didn't recognize the tune but that wasn't unusual with school band. As she listened, however, the music began to remind her of Christmas and ice and candy.

"That's it," thought Swimming Pool, snapping her fingers, "the snowflake song!" Without realizing it, she was counting waltz-time under her breath, "One-two-three, one-two-three—"

At the time, Swimming Pool was alone in the hall. The linoleum floor gave off a shiny gloss from a recent waxing. She lifted Fred in one arm so he could hear the music and then she positioned her other arm as Miss Ginger had instructed. She closed her eyes and began marking a small Box Step. Left-right-left, right-left-right. And before long, Swimming Pool and the lobster were taking a little waltz around the hall. Her high-tops squeaked against the linoleum, more or less in rhythm. But after a few more snowflakes, Swimming Pool heard a noise that shattered the moment. She froze on the spot. From the far end of the hallway, someone had cleared his throat. Swimming Pool was totally busted.

She looked up to find Ernie, smiling broadly and clapping his hands. "The Box Step," said Ernie. "I recognize that dance! It's the Box Step!"

"Knock it off, Ernie," Swimming said, balling up a fist for good measure.

Ernie came closer and bent over the water fountain for a slurp. "Hey, Fred," said Ernie, wiping his mouth. As usual, Fred didn't answer. "Hey, Pool," said Ernie. "Long time no."

Swimming Pool was tempted not to answer. She was tempted to walk away without a word. But instead she said, "I'm not talking to you, Ernie."

Ernie grimaced. "Okay," he said. "Be that way. I'm not talking to you either."

"So then what are you doing talking to me?" asked Swimming Pool.

Ernie couldn't argue with that logic. He waved his hands and turned to walk away.

But Swimming Pool couldn't bear not dealing with the subject while she had the chance. So she went ahead and brought it up. "I can't believe you like me," she said.

Ernie stopped in the hall and slowly turned around. "I don't like you," he said.

"Well, I don't like you either," said Swimming Pool. "But you told somebody you liked me."

"I never told anybody I liked you," Ernie protested.

"Then how come they say you like me?"

"How am I supposed to know?" Ernie threw his hands up in frustration. It was as if a four-hundred-pound gorilla was sitting between them holding a valentine that neither of them had ordered.

"Just so you know," said Swimming Pool, going for the last word, "I never liked you."

"Me neither," said Ernie.

"Okay."

"So okay."

It was quiet between them for a moment. Then Ernie asked, "You swear you didn't write the note in glitter?"

"Ernie," said Swimming Pool, "we did glitter in art class and I just about flunked!"

Both Ernie and Swimming Pool snickered about that.

"So are we still friends?" Ernie asked.

Swimming Pool hesitated slightly. "Who says we're not friends?" she said.

Ernie was still confused. "But it doesn't make sense. How do we stay friends and let everybody know we don't like each other and still stay friends?"

"Wow," said Swimming Pool. "You're too heavy for me."

Ernie looked from left to right. The hall was still empty. They both still had hall passes and a little time to kill. Ernie figured this was as good a time as any to bring up the subject of baseball.

"So you okay?" he asked. "We miss you on the team."

"Tell it to my mom," said Swimming Pool. "You were there. I got thrown out of charm school. Miss Ginger called me uncouth!"

"What's 'uncouth'?" said Ernie.

"How am I supposed to know?" groused Swimming Pool. "But it doesn't sound like a gold star to me!"

Ernie was reluctant to address the consequences of the charm school debacle but he figured it was now or never. "So no more birthday party?" he ventured. "No baseball?"

"Think about it," said Swimming Pool. "I've got so

much free time I'll probably make straight A's."

"I'm sorry, Swimming Pool," said Ernie. "I'm really sorry." They stood in the hall for a moment without making a noise. They didn't fidget. Even the linoleum was quiet.

Swimming Pool sighed and shook her head. "I don't know what to do," she said. She reached for Fred, ready to head back to class.

Ernie turned slowly as the idea brewed in his head. "Hold it," he said. "Hold it a minute." He paced back and forth in the hall as he thought out loud. "Your mom said no baseball and no birthday party unless you get through charm school. Is that correct?"

"That's what she said," said Swimming Pool.

"Did she say it had to be a specific charm school?"

"Miss Ginger's School of Tap & Tumbling," Swimming Pool said with a shrug. "Where else is there?"

Ernie didn't answer at first. But he smiled. It was the smile he used when he had just concocted a brilliant scheme. "Uh-oh," thought Swimming Pool. "What now?"

Ernie laid out his idea as if he had opened up a box and was pulling out a string of pearls. "Who's to say," he began, "we can't start our own charm school?"

"Our own charm school?" Swimming Pool repeated, suddenly incredulous and shrill. "Ernie, you'll forgive me, but I think of you and 'charm' isn't the first word that comes to mind."

"I got charm to spare," Ernie replied. "I am oozing with charm."

"But where are we going to have it?" Swimming Pool asked, challenging Ernie to get down to business.

"What's wrong with the Moose Lodge?" said Ernie.

"I thought that place was haunted."

"It's creepy but it's nice."

"But who's going to throw the party?" asked Swimming Pool. "We'd have to have decorations and punch and—"

Swimming Pool didn't even reach the word "cookies" before she saw where Ernie was headed.

"Dusty," they said together.

"Would Dusty do it?" Swimming Pool asked.

"Who knows?" said Ernie. "Can't hurt to ask."

"He'll do it for me," said Swimming Pool. "I'll ask."

"No, I'll ask," said Ernie. "Dusty and I have unfinished business."

"Suit yourself," said Swimming Pool. She knew about the unfinished business. She was relieved that Ernie was prepared to sort it out. "But what about music? What about invitations?"

"So many questions," said Ernie. "It always works out!"

"And who are we going to invite? Who's going to attend? All the girls I know go to Miss Ginger's! Why would anybody come to our charm school when they all go to Miss Ginger's?"

"We'll get *boys*," said Ernie. "We'll tell them we got boys."

"Boys?" Swimming Pool was dumbstruck. She was shocked at such a good idea. She was so shocked that it just about knocked the wind out of her. "Oh, that's good," she said. "But where are we going to find boys?"

"Swimming Pool," said Ernie, like she was really dense. "Between you and me and the baseball team, we got boys."

Swimming Pool shook her head and chuckled. She had to admit that was true.

"Besides," Ernie continued, "people owe me favors and I know people owe you."

This was true too. Swimming Pool didn't like to think that people owed her favors. But she admitted that it was probably true.

"So okay, Ernie," she said. "We throw this party and tell the girls we got boys. That's still not charm school! That's just a boy-girl party! Who are we going to get to teach us about manners, charm, and etiquette? All that stuff!"

"Etiquette," Ernie repeated. "Grandma stuff, right?"

"Basically, but it's tricky," said Swimming Pool. "There are rules, rules, lots of rules."

Ernie sighed. He was stumped. He tapped his foot. He went for another drink of water but Fred was still hogging the fountain.

"Fred!" Ernie thought. The answer was staring him in the face.

"Fred!" Ernie cried out loud, grabbing the lobster in his hand. "We'll use Fred! Kids love learning the Rules of Fred."

"Fred!" cried Swimming Pool, suddenly reunited with a long lost friend. "That's perfect!"

"Except it won't be etiquette anymore," said Ernie, handing her the lobster. "It'll be Freddy-quette."

Swimming Pool laughed. "I don't know, Ernie," she said warily. "We still don't have anybody to teach us to dance. It isn't charm school unless we make the kids dance. And we can't ask Miss Ginger. I'm afraid of Miss Ginger. Who do we know who can dance?"

"Tony?" said Ernie.

"Not Tony," said Swimming Pool. "He's too expensive. Besides, I got my pride."

Ernie smiled. He had to admit, though, that Swimming

Pool had a point. Without a dance teacher, they might as well give up on the idea. They could throw a party, sure. But it wouldn't be charm school unless they could think of someone who knew how to dance.

And who did he know who could dance?

The answer should have been obvious but it still took Ernie by surprise. In fact, when the answer came, he closed his eyes and smiled. The answer was so obvious it had snuck up and whacked him in the head.

"I got it," said Ernie. "Don't worry, I got it."

"Who?" said Swimming Pool. "Not Miss Ginger. I told you. I'm afraid of Miss Ginger."

"Don't worry," Ernie repeated. "I'll get us a dance teacher. You can leave it to me."

At that moment, Mr. Fowler, the assistant principal, growled "Hey!" from the far end of the hall, sounding a lot meaner than both Swimming Pool and Ernie actually knew him to be. "You kids better have a hall pass!"

"It's okay, Mr. Fowler," said Ernie, holding up his piece of wood. Swimming Pool held up Fred and waved his little claw. Mr. Fowler eyed the lobster and nodded okay.

But it would be quite some time before that lobster would ever be seen again.

CHAPTER NINETEEN

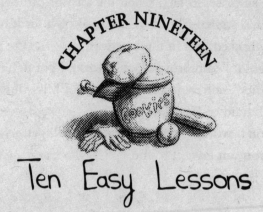

Ten Easy Lessons

There was a new sign affixed to the gate outside Cat Lady's house. It read: "Beware of Kitty."

"More like 'Beware of kitty litter,'" Ernie said as he pushed past the gate and into Cat Lady's yard.

Ernie wasn't afraid of Cat Lady's cats. In the time since Cat Lady had become a friend, she would often ask Ernie to feed her cats whenever she left town. He was in the habit of giving a merry little whistle whenever he walked through the gate to let the cats know he'd arrived and watch them come running.

"Who's whistling in my yard?" Cat Lady growled from the porch.

"Oh, hey," said Ernie. "I didn't see you there. I was just stopping by to say Hi."

"You were just stopping by to torture my cats," said Cat Lady. "Knock it off with the whistle."

"They like it," said Ernie. "They recognize me."

"You may think they recognize you," said Cat Lady, "but I got news for you. Cats don't think. You know what this one's thinking right now?" she asked. She scruffed the neck of the tabby cat she was holding.

Ernie scrunched his face. "What?"

Cat Lady pursed her lips and buzzed like the static on the television when the cable goes down. "White noise," she said. "The power's on, but nothing's there."

"If that's the case," Ernie asked, "how come this one likes me and that one doesn't?" He pointed to the black cat curling between his legs and the calico on the ledge that couldn't be bothered.

"Just chemistry," said Cat Lady. "Go figure."

Cat Lady dropped the tabby cat to the ground and it fussed and mewed at her. Cat Lady fussed and mewed right back. She and the cats spoke the same language. "Who's a fussy cat?" Cat Lady said. "Who's a fussy cat?"

"Keep it up," said Ernie. "People already think you're crazy." He followed Cat Lady past the front door and into her living room where she appeared to be in the middle of an afternoon cup of tea.

"I know, I'm 'Cat Lady,'" she groaned. "As if I care what other people think. I like cats. Everybody knows it. So what?" Two Siamese cats appeared from the hall. They wandered between her legs and coiled their tails around her ankles. "I've been trying to downsize," Cat Lady admitted, flopping onto the sofa, "but how can I pick which one goes when I love them all?!"

Ernie watched as one Siamese cat settled on her lap. The other Siamese cat crawled onto the crook of her elbow.

Ernie had intended to ask Cat Lady if she'd help out with charm school, of course, but he had been meaning to talk to her about something else as well. He didn't expect the opportunity to present itself so easily—but when it did, he figured there was no time like the present. So, quite out of the blue, he went ahead and asked.

"You like my dad, don't you?" That was the question on his mind.

Cat Lady arched an eyebrow ever so slightly, but then she continued as though Ernie's question was completely reasonable.

"I do like your father," she said, enthusiastically. "He's got a good personality, a good sense of humor, and if he says he's going to do something, he does it." She juggled the Siamese and a teacup in one arm as she reached for a slice of lemon. "Your father is a nice man," she added as if to close the subject.

Ernie interrupted. "I don't mean like good neighbors," he said, "I mean like boyfriend-girlfriend. I mean like going-on-dates."

"Oh, yeah, yes, well," said Cat Lady, pausing to blow on her tea, "I figured that's what you were getting at."

"So I was right," Ernie concluded.

"Hold your horses," said Cat Lady. "Your father and I are friends. It doesn't have to mean anything. We like each other. We spend time together. We enjoy each other's company."

"Are you guys going to warn me?" Ernie asked.

Cat Lady arched an eyebrow again ever so slightly. Ernie was full of surprises today. "Warn you about what?" she asked.

"Warn me if things are getting romantic," he said.

Cat Lady held onto a mouthful of tea and placed her teacup down while she took the time to swallow. "Ernie," she began to say, but Ernie interrupted.

"Things are already romantic, aren't they?" he said. "I watch TV, I've seen movies. I'm not an idiot. Grown-ups spend time together but when it's a man and woman, it's never really just friends."

"You're friends with Swimming Pool," Cat Lady argued.

Ernie scoffed. "Just barely," he said.

"Oh, what happened now?" groaned Cat Lady as though the dramas in this neighborhood were the greatest story ever told. She was also eager to change the subject.

Ernie sighed before spilling the beans. "It's just that kids heard about this note I found in my backpack and started saying Swimming Pool wrote it. They started saying she likes me."

"Well, does she?" said Cat Lady.

"Not like that!" said Ernie.

"So why did she write you a note?"

"She didn't write it!" protested Ernie. "I don't know who wrote it. It wasn't signed. It's just a piece of yellow paper I found folded up and tucked in the little zipper pocket of my backpack. Like the pocket you never use."

Cat Lady was quiet for a moment. "What did it say?" she asked.

"Well that's the weird thing," Ernie continued. "It doesn't say anything. It's just words written in glitter."

"Glitter?" said Cat Lady.

Ernie was relieved that Cat Lady seemed to think that was weird. "Right," he said, "like how weird is that?"

Cat Lady took a sip of tea and carefully swallowed. "So what does it say?" she asked.

Ernie threw his hands on his hips to deliver the punch line. "I know who likes you," he said and waited for a response.

Ernie thought the extreme weirdness of it all would get a bigger rise out of Cat Lady but she didn't say a thing. She placed her teacup down, pursed her lips, and looked away.

"Isn't that weird?" Ernie asked, pushing for a reaction.

To his surprise, Cat Lady responded with a gentle frown. "Have you asked your dad about this note?" she said.

"Forget about it," said Ernie, rolling his eyes. "How stupid do I look?"

"Ask your dad," Cat Lady said, like that was a really good idea. "You can do what you want, but I think you should ask your dad."

Ernie shrugged okay. He was a little disappointed that the note was still such a mystery but it wasn't anything he needed to solve today. He was just about to change the subject to charm school when he realized that Cat Lady still hadn't answered his question.

"So what's the story? Do you like my dad?"

Cat Lady was back on the hook. "I'll let you know," she said. "Give me a little time. But I'll let you know."

"Fair enough," said Ernie with a shrug.

Ernie stood up, ready to leave, but then he realized he'd never asked Cat Lady about charm school.

"Oh!" he said. "I still have to ask you a favor."

"A favor?" Cat Lady groaned. "What now?"

"I'm starting a charm school," he said, like that was the most natural thing in the world. "And I need somebody to teach us how to dance. You know how to dance, right?"

"Dance? What kind of dance?"

"Boy-girl stuff. Old-fashioned stuff. 'May I have this dance?' That kind of dance."

"You mean like Ten Easy Lessons?" said Cat Lady, imitating a television commercial. "Ten Easy Lessons and you too will know how to dance?"

"Not exactly," said Ernie. "You don't get ten lessons, you only get one. This is a one-shot charm school. But this is nothing you can't handle, believe me. I've seen you dance. You're a good dancer."

Cat Lady smiled. It took less than a moment for her to answer "Okay."

"Okay?" said Ernie. "That's it? You'll do it?"

"I said Okay."

"So what do you charge?" Ernie asked.

"I'm not going to charge anything," said Cat Lady. "This one is for free. It's only one lesson, right? If it was ten, that would cost you a bundle."

"Just one easy lesson," said Ernie. "You got a deal." He reached out to shake Cat Lady's hand. The kitty on Cat Lady's arm didn't know what was happening as she reached out for the handshake but it went along for the ride.

"My pleasure," said Cat Lady. "Thanks for asking."

"No, please," said Ernie. "The pleasure is mine." He got up to leave but paused before he hit the door.

"Cat Lady?" he said. She looked up from the couch.

Both of the Siamese looked too. Ernie smiled and shrugged and then he continued.

"I just want you to know that I appreciate what you have to offer."

The door to Dusty's toolshed had been painted solid white. In big black letters, Dusty had written a message on the door. It read: "This is not a door."

Ernie read the message two or three times and he still didn't understand what it meant. He opened the door and peered into the darkness. "Dusty?" he said.

"Ernie?" said Dusty. "Whoa, this is a surprise. Long time no. Long time no."

As usual, Dusty was sitting at his worktable. He put down a paintbrush and wiped his hands on a rag. Several different containers were spread across the table—clay pots, plastic buckets, and large tin cans in various stages of decoration.

"What's the new project?" said Ernie.

"Cookie jars," said Dusty, nodding eagerly. "I'm expanding on my peanut butter cookie thing."

Ernie nodded two or three times as well. "Well, that makes sense," he said.

Dusty didn't gesture for Ernie to sit down but Ernie went ahead and sat down anyway.

"Hey, what's up with the door?" he asked.

"What do you mean?" said Dusty.

Ernie recited the message: "This is not a door."

"Oh, that's old," Dusty laughed. "That's been up there for a while."

"But what does it mean?" asked Ernie.

Dusty shrugged. "I like to make people think," he said. "I'll probably paint over it tomorrow." Dusty reached for his paintbrush to go back to work.

"So Dusty," Ernie began, not knowing where to begin.

"So you want to start a charm school," said Dusty.

"How did you know?" said Ernie, taken by surprise. "Did Swimming Pool tell you?"

"She didn't have to tell me," said Dusty. "In the old days, you would have been all gung-ho about starting a charm school from the moment she said she had to go."

"Score one for Dusty," thought Ernie. But "Whoa, whoa, whoa," is what he said. "I have been very busy lately, in case you haven't noticed."

"I know," said Dusty. "You've got all your fancy new baseball friends."

"You're on the baseball team too, Dusty."

"But I'm not popular the way you are."

"Go figure," said Ernie. "Kids had to practically beg you to let them help paint that wall. It's a two-way street, Dusty. Friendship can be complicated. Very complicated."

Dusty couldn't argue with that.

"So will you help?" Ernie asked. "With charm school?"

Dusty shook his head. "The only time I ever see you, Ernie," he said, "is when you need a favor."

"That's not true," said Ernie. "I see you at practice. I see you at games."

"That doesn't count," said Dusty.

"I run into you in the cafeteria every now and then."

Dusty threw a look as though that answer was truly

pathetic. "I'm happy to do favors," said Dusty. "But I do favors for friends. And in the friend department, you have been very disappointing, I got to say."

Ernie felt like he'd been punched in the stomach. He hated it when people told him they were disappointed in him.

"I hate to say it," said Dusty, "but it's the truth. Terribly, terribly disappointed."

Ernie rose from the bench. "You got some nerve," he said to Dusty. "You're disappointed in me? Well, I'm disappointed in you. You're the one who told the school about the note in glitter. Don't pretend it didn't happen."

Dusty cringed. "That was an accident," he said.

"Right, an accident," said Ernie. "Thanks a lot, Benedict Arnold."

"I can explain," said Dusty. "Ronjon was being nice to me. You weren't. He was helping me paint the wall. I was upset that day because you had called me weird. So I told Ronjon about your name-calling and I said how you were one to talk. That's when I told him about the note in glitter 'cause it had seemed so weird at the time."

Ernie nodded, remembering the unpleasant scene at the pitcher's mound. He probably would have done the same thing. "I never thought the story would go so far out of control," Dusty added with regret.

Ernie took in Dusty's story. He also took in the sights and smells of Dusty's workroom. It had always been such a pleasure to hang out here with Dusty, hashing through problems and fixing the world.

Outside the workshop, things got more complicated. Ernie had made new friends, like Kip, who took up his time.

It sounded like Dusty was making new friends with Ronjon, Marcus, and Noah Morgenstern. And Swimming Pool, well, Swimming Pool knew everybody. "How do friendships get so messed up?" said Ernie. "We were good friends, Dusty. I don't know how we fell out of touch. It's hard holding onto friends when everybody's growing up so fast."

"I'm not growing up fast," said Dusty. "I was a runt when you met me and I'm still a runt now."

Ernie laughed. "I'm sorry I said you were weird," he said to Dusty.

"No, you're not," Dusty replied. "You just want to get me to come up with ideas for your charm school."

"Well, sure," said Ernie. "But I'm sorry it upset you. I'm not really sorry you're weird because if you weren't so weird, I wouldn't want you to build the charm school."

"Is that supposed to be a compliment?" asked Dusty.

"Whatever," said Ernie. "I'm sorry you're weird and I'm glad you're weird. Both at the same time."

Dusty laughed. "Ernie," he said, shaking his head, "you could sell lunch to the lunch lady."

Ernie laughed. "Help us out, Dusty," he said, spreading his arms. "We need you. If you don't say yes, we'll have to go ask Noah Morgenstern."

Dusty didn't say yes or no. He simply got to work. "So what are you thinking for charm school?" he said, reaching for an empty pad and a thick black marker. "We need a theme."

"You're the one with the ideas," said Ernie. "But nothing stupid. Miss Ginger's charm school was fun but it was b-i-g on stupid. Let's make it something smart."

"Something smart," Dusty repeated. Then suddenly, his eyes lit up. "Something smart, something smart!"

"What'd I say?" said Ernie. But Dusty had already jumped from his worktable to dig through several boxes.

"Ernie, you're a genius!" said Dusty with his head buried in odds and ends and who knows what.

Ernie shrugged. "I am?" he observed. "What do you know? A genius and I don't even know it."

CHAPTER TWENTY

The Brainiac Ball

Invitations to the Brainiac Ball featured the names of Ernie, Swimming Pool, and Dusty so that all the kids in the neighborhood would know that the old team was back in business.

The invitations also specified that the guests should "Dress Smart"—and kids really went all out for the event. Some dressed in their very best clothes with added zingers like top hats and boas. Others went out on a limb and showed up as wizards, explorers, diplomats, or computer geeks. There were mad scientists, surgeons, and maestros. Psychiatrists and swamis.

Gina arrived wearing a long white lab coat that most kids recognized from school. Betty carried a briefcase and a cell phone and wore her mother's "power pearls." Kirsten carried a karaoke microphone and went person to person with probing questions, nodding earnestly through the answers. Finny and Fanny wore black turtlenecks and French berets and spent the evening speaking in rhyming couplets like bad poets.

"Such a smart choice," everyone said when they noticed someone's costume. "Now that was a smart thing to wear."

Everyone had a big laugh when Noah Morgenstern arrived dressed like a lightbulb. "What a bright idea," Dusty had to admit.

Dusty occupied a table at the door and made sure that everyone received a name badge. It was a sticker that said "Hello My Name Is . . ."—but in the blank that followed Dusty had written the name of one of the Moose members or the Daughters of the American Revolution from the composite photos inside. They were old-fashioned, dinosaur names, like Otto and Imogene, so that guests could launch themselves into the party by introducing themselves as someone else entirely.

"Hello! My name is Abigail Turnberry!" said Swimming Pool, as she greeted Kip at the door. She extended her palm and they shook hands enthusiastically.

Kip was dressed as an astronaut for the event. "Hello, Miss Abigail," he replied. He referred to his own name badge and continued with gusto. "My name is Isaac Klemstock and I'd like to introduce my friend Clarence Mulrooney." He turned slightly to acknowledge Ronjon as he wandered wide-eyed up the stairs. Ronjon was wearing a fright wig and a cardigan sweater.

"Good evening, Clarence!" said Swimming Pool. Then she added under her breath, "Who are you supposed to be?"

"Albert Einstein," said Ronjon. "But my name is Clarence Mulrooney tonight."

As the guests ascended the Moose Lodge stairs, some paused to find their namesakes on the composite photos. "There I am!" a voice would cry. Other kids steamrolled ahead, pushing through all the introductions with acquaintances and friends. Already there was a lot of lively chatter.

At the top of the stairs was a big surprise. Dusty and a crew of Comets had completely transformed the hall. The walls were covered in complicated math problems written in several shades of colored sidewalk chalk. Dusty had consulted Gina so that he knew the math was good. Overhead, big goofy balloons were clustered in clumps from the ceiling— but they weren't balloons at all. They were surgical gloves, inflated into giant hands. Flags of many nations billowed from posts. Party streamers crisscrossed the space, but on closer inspection, it was actually several strands of measuring tape, knotted end to end.

Above the dance floor, a long, clear hose did a complicated loop-the-loop through the rafters. Somehow, it was filled with green slime that gurgled and slurped like a science experiment run amock. Kids cried, "Gross!" from the dance floor but it still looked cool all the same.

A bevy of tables and chairs skirted the large dance floor. The tables were covered with big sheets of butcher paper. Dusty had used thick black markers to write brain teasers on the paper—like "If you take two apples from three apples, how many do you have?" Chemistry beakers were filled with crayons so that kids could write down answers. In the center of each table was a tower of library books that had freshly picked flowers stuck between the pages.

Tony was manning the Moose Lodge boom box. Dusty

decided it was best to let Tony choose all the music himself but he did say that "It would be nice if a lot of the songs included the word 'think.'"

As the guests found their seats, everyone agreed that Dusty had outdone himself again with the Brainiac Ball. But once they were seated, Dusty pulled another surprise. Slide projectors had been positioned in the far corners of the room and they cast images of great wonders on all four walls. Kids facing west saw Big Ben, the Taj Mahal, and the Eiffel Tower. Kids facing east saw the Great Pyramids, the Sphinx, and the Colosseum.

Gina and the girl with braids and braces played a guessing game to see who could name all the famous places. "The Great Wall of China, the Leaning Tower of Pisa, and the Great Barrier Reef," said the girl with braids and braces. "The Hoover Dam, the Empire State Building, and the Suez Canal," said Gina.

Refreshments, naturally, consisted of brain food. "Nuts and berries and natural sugars," said Dusty, "except of course for the—"

"Peanut butter cookies," he and Swimming Pool said in unison.

Red and Cat Lady each accepted a peanut butter cookie as Gina passed them, carrying a tray. They had been invited to attend the event as official chaperones. So far, the job meant three peanut butter cookies and two cups of punch.

Ernie made a point of inviting Swimming Pool's mom but Swimming Pool insisted that she not be given any responsibility. "Like she can't be an official chaperone," Swimming Pool said. "She can't be working. She's there to see me graduate from charm school. She has to believe that charm school is for real."

As it was, Swimming Pool's mom stood on the sidelines of the Brainiac Ball, slightly bewildered by the splendor of it all. She was nibbling a cookie and sipping a glass of punch with Red and Cat Lady. "How did that all happen?" she asked, gesturing at the room.

"It was Dusty," said Red.

"And Ernie," Cat Lady offered.

"And Swimming Pool," added Red.

Swimming Pool's mom shook her head as if she had no idea such a thing was possible.

Ernie, Dusty, and Swimming Pool looked over the room and felt pretty good about themselves. The place looked great and everyone was having a good time.

"Are we all set with Fred?" asked Ernie.

"I'll go check," said Swimming Pool. "Are we all set with Cat Lady?"

"I'll go check," said Ernie.

"Uh-oh," said Dusty. "We got a problem."

"What's the matter?" said Ernie and Swimming Pool at the same time.

Dusty pointed at the room. For some reason, even though there was plenty of chatter—and everyone seemed to be having a good time—all the boys were sitting with boys and all the girls were sitting with girls. No one was sitting together. Swimming Pool freaked. "We got too much riding on this charm school to have it tank," she said.

"What do we do?" said Ernie.

"We got to break the ice," said Swimming Pool.

"We don't need ice," said Dusty. "The punch is cold."

"Not that kind of ice," said Swimming Pool. "It's just an expression."

But before she could explain further, Swimming Pool had charged among the tables, mingling from table to table. She gestured for Dusty to do the same—although Dusty wasn't exactly sure what he was expected to do.

"Um, hi," said Dusty, as he leaned over a table where Finny and Fanny sat with the girl with the braces and braids. He looked at Swimming Pool, who was already waving at him from two tables away. She was pulling Ronjon from his chair and sending him across the room.

"I'm sending over Ronjon," Swimming Pool signaled in sign. "He's supposed to get braces and his mom and aunt are twins."

"Good thinking," Dusty signaled back.

Before long, Dusty was signaling Swimming Pool about Noah Morganstern's new pet hamster and sending him over to sit with Gina. "Good work," signaled Swimming Pool. "Keep 'em coming!"

Once the room was balanced between boys and girls, Ernie signaled for Tony to lower the music. He stepped onstage with Kirsten's karaoke microphone. "Ladies and gentlemen," he announced, "I hate to interrupt your fun and games, but we do have a little matter of etiquette to cover tonight. Otherwise, it would never be called charm school. I know you'll be patient while we run through a few rules—and to assist us in this matter, we have none other than that celebrated stickler for the very best table manners. Ladies and gentlemen, I give you—Fred!"

With that cue, the Comets began drumming on any available surface. Their collective effort added up to quite a drumroll. There was a buzz in the room as kids tried to figure out if they had just heard what they thought they'd just heard. Heads turned in every direction to try and see where Fred, that frisky lobster, might be.

And then, quite miraculously, Fred was slowly lowered from the ceiling. He was housed in a silver aquarium that shimmered in the light. The kids, of course, went wild.

Ernie approached the lobster tank with Kirsten's karaoke microphone and asked Fred if there was anything he wanted to say. He held the microphone over the lobster tank.

To everyone's surprise, Fred began to talk.

> It doesn't matter
> Whose house you're in.
> Use your fork
> And wipe your chin.

It was only Swimming Pool, of course, pinching her nose and reading into an offstage microphone. Even so, kids were crazy about the New Rules of Fred.

> It's good at a party
> To raise a toast.
> And never forget
> To thank the host.

Fred went on for several more stanzas. There seemed to

be more Rules of Fred than there ever had been before. But no one seemed to mind because Fred was so funny.

Fred pulled a pop quiz and made all the children write three important things about manners onto the butcher paper that served as tablecloths. Then Fred admonished them with one final poem:

> If you use your best manners,
> A good time will be had.
> But if you act rude,
> Face it. You're a crab.

All the kids laughed as Fred was hoisted back up to the ceiling. They chattered among themselves, wondering what would happen next, when Ernie returned to the stage.

"Time for the dance lesson portion of our charm school," he announced, "but I promise you, no Box Step, no triangle step—no rectangles either!"

The kids laughed easily. Backstage, Swimming Pool smiled. Ernie was learning how to work a crowd.

"We are going to teach you how to dance in one easy lesson," Ernie continued, "which is going to be delivered by none other than—" He waved his arm dramatically toward the wings, as he concluded, "—Ms. Warren!"

The audience gasped at the sight as Cat Lady stormed onto the stage. They stared blankly as Cat Lady grabbed the microphone out of Ernie's hand. But Cat Lady didn't seem perturbed in the least. In fact, Cat Lady was a lot of fun.

"Oh, right," said Cat Lady into the microphone. "Ms. Warren, who's that?" She smirked and did a little curtsy at

Ernie. "Call me Cat Lady," she continued with a smile. "I know you already do!"

From the back of the room, Ronjon yelled, "Cat Lady!"

"That's not very loud," said Cat Lady. "Can't you do better than that?"

"Cat Lady!" cried Ronjon, Kip, and the girl with braces and braids.

Soon enough, Cat Lady had all the kids shouting "Cat Lady" at the top of their lungs. And not long after that, she had all the kids on their feet and on the dance floor. She dispensed with the obligation of having to dance with a partner.

"I want everyone facing me!" Cat Lady said. "In straight lines, like a grid!"

"Uh-oh," said Swimming Pool. "I thought Ernie said no geometry." But Swimming Pool's fears were soon dispelled when Tony cranked up the music and Cat Lady announced that they were going to learn "a simple old-fashioned line dance called the Electric Slide."

The dance consisted of extremely basic steps and claps except for one tricky pivot in the middle when you had to know what you were doing. Other than that, the dance was easy, easy, easy. Betty could do it, Gina could do it, and even Noah Morgenstern could do it. Tony threw in his own personal moves and Kip surprised everyone with a few moves of his own. The first song was still playing and Cat Lady already had the entire room laughing, dancing, and begging for more of the Electric Slide.

When the dancing had reached its peak and the party was

ready to slide into gift-bags and good-byes, Ernie walked onto the stage with Kirsten's karaoke microphone for one final announcement. "I'd like everybody's attention, please," he said.

A rumble of laughter traveled across the room as the kids realized that Ernie was now wearing a graduation cap and gown. Except Ernie's cap was a baseball cap with a mortarboard stuck on top of it.

"It's time for a very special moment in our festivities," said Ernie. He reached for the tassel dangling off the mortarboard as he continued, "It's time to graduate from charm school!" A cheer rose up as Ernie flipped the tassel over to the other side of his mortarboard.

"When I recite your name," said Ernie, "would you kindly approach the stage to accept your diploma?" Most of the kids were familiar with the graduation drill from kindergarten. Dusty stepped onstage with what appeared to be a stack of paper plates and stood there ceremoniously beside Ernie, waiting for the first name.

Naturally, the first name was "Swimming Pool."

A cheer of relief rose from the crowd. Ronjon and Kip began a chant that sounded like barking dogs. Swimming Pool let out a hoot herself and fairly ran from the back of the room. She was so excited that she skipped the steps and hopped right onto the stage.

Red and Cat Lady laughed and applauded. Swimming Pool's mom raised a disposable camera so that she'd be ready to take the photo at precisely the right moment.

Ernie held out his hand for the congratulatory handshake and Swimming Pool snagged it. Dusty handed Ernie a paper plate and, after one fake-out maneuver, Ernie passed it to Swimming Pool.

Swimming Pool's mom warbled with excitement. She clicked a photo and the camera went flash.

Swimming Pool looked down at the paper plate. In a swirl of yarn, glue, and colored marker, it read: "Congratulations, Swimming Pool. Your charm school diploma!"

CHAPTER TWENTY-ONE

Home and Away

The Comets ended up losing the regional championships but nobody was too upset about it. The critical game against the Army Girls was played at the Army Girls' ballpark and, unfortunately, the stadium really wasn't very nice. In fact, midgame, the Comets agreed that the only reason they were performing so poorly was that the Army Girls' ballpark was such a dump.

"Like they couldn't slap this joint with a coat of paint?" Ronjon cried. "This dump isn't nearly as nice as home." Everyone in the dugout muttered in agreement.

Ernie smiled. He hadn't thought of the Comets' ballpark as "home" before but, of course, it made perfect sense. "Home and away," he thought. "If this is away, that must be home."

And even if they did lose against the Army Girls, the

Comets were soon distracted by the prospects of Swimming Pool's birthday party.

Swimming Pool had asked Dusty to help out with the arrangements, of course. She really had no choice after Dusty's huge success with the Brainiac Ball.

"But please," Swimming Pool begged. "Something simple, Dusty. Simple, simple, simple."

"I can do simple," Dusty piped.

Ernie and Swimming Pool exchanged a look and burst into laughter.

In truth, Dusty made good on his word. It took a little talking and a little self-control but Dusty managed to organize the eleventh birhtday party that Swimming Pool had always wanted.

It was a pool party.

On the one hand, this should have been easy because Swimming Pool's parents already had a pool. Unfortunately, it was a tremendous, outdoor, above-ground contraption that held a gazillion gallons of water. And it was currently stored in the garage.

Swimming Pool told Dusty that her dad swore he would never put it up again after her brothers had gone berserk during a Fourth of July barbecue. Swimming Pool's dad had a reputation for laying down the law.

"Swimming Pool," said Dusty, "you only turn eleven once! If you want a pool party, you should have a pool party!"

"You don't know my mom and dad!" Swimming Pool protested. "It's okay if it doesn't happen. They're not going to want to bring out the swimming pool!"

Dusty shook his hands and imitated the "Whoosh, whoosh, whoosh." "Trust me, Pool," he said. "I know how to talk to moms."

And so it happened that Dusty stopped by Swimming Pool's house with a plate of fresh peanut butter cookies for Swimming Pool's mom. "Oh, Dusty!" she said with surprise when she found him standing on her doorstep.

"Oh, Dusty!" she said again, but in a different tone altogether, when Dusty mentioned his plans for Swimming Pool's birthday party. The pool was an issue, of course, but Swimming Pool's mom was also concerned about Dusty staging a Brainiac Ball on her back porch. "I don't know, Dusty," she fretted, reaching into the refrigerator for the jug of milk to go with the cookies.

Dusty took the opportunity to pull Swimming Pool's charm school diploma off the refrigerator door. He changed the subject from Swimming Pool's birthday party altogether. Instead, he prattled on and on about the wonderful impact that charm school seemed to have on Swimming Pool. "She's a changed girl," said Dusty. "I see it! Don't you?"

"Oh, yes," said Swimming Pool's mom. "Yes, yes."

"Like her sincerity and compassion," said Dusty. He tried to list all those qualities about Swimming Pool that charm school had not damaged.

Swimming Pool's mom completely agreed. And while they were in such close agreement, Dusty commented on the fragile hopes and dreams of any girl who was about to turn eleven. "Like good friends and loyalty," said Dusty.

"Oh, yes, yes," said Swimming Pool's mom.

"And the chance to have a really cool boy-girl pool party," Dusty added in a rush. Swimming Pool's mom blinked once or twice, but she kept listening.

And whatever Dusty said, it worked. By the time he left Swimming Pool's house, Swimming Pool's mom had not only agreed on the pool party, she insisted on it.

"George, put up the pool!" she shouted at Swimming Pool's dad before Dusty was even out the door.

Red was banging around the kitchen as Ernie got ready for the pool party.

"Another party?" asked Red. "What is it with you guys? Party, party, party!"

"Hoo-hoo!" Ernie crowed as he tucked his swimsuit, a mask, and a snorkel into his backpack. "Happy Birthday, Swimming Pool!" Ernie was careful not to crush the highly collectible set of baseball cards that he was giving Swimming Pool as a birthday present so he moved them to the the zippered pocket in front.

That was when Ernie remembered about the note in glitter. And his question about Cat Lady.

"Hey, Dad," Ernie said, flinging his backpack onto a kitchen stool. "We need to talk."

"Talk about what?" said Red. He was preoccupied with

the instructions on a package of macaroni and cheese. A pot of water was already perched on a hot burner.

"Well, Cat Lady," said Ernie, cutting to the chase.

Red arched his eyebrows and put the box down. "What about Cat Lady?" he asked. "And the name is Catherine. Catherine Warren."

"I like her," said Ernie. "I like her fine. But I'm not ready for a new mom or anything like that."

Although it took a moment for that remark to sink in, Red didn't seem particularly thrown by it. "Nobody's going to replace your mom," he said. "I'm not looking for anybody to replace your mom. Cat Lady—I mean, Catherine and I— we're just friends."

"I know," Ernie said with mock disgust. "'We're just friends!' That's what she said."

"She said? Said when?"

"When I went to ask her to teach us to dance."

"You went to her house to have some little talk?" Red sounded slightly nervous.

"Dad," Ernie protested, "I feed the lady's cats from time to time. This is not so unusual."

The water on the burner had started to boil. Red turned it off. "So what'd she say?" he asked.

"She says you're a nice man," said Ernie. He reached into a box and chomped on a cracker.

"Nice?" Red repeated. "Is that all?"

"This is not about you, Dad," said Ernie, reaching into his backpack. "Cat Lady told me to ask you about this." Ernie pulled out the note in glitter and pushed it across the counter toward Red.

"What is it?" Red asked.

"It's a note in glitter," said Ernie. "Read it."

Red opened the note and read the message inside. "'I know who likes you,'" said Ernie. He could recite it by heart.

"Where did this come from?" Red asked.

"Dad," Ernie said peevishly, like he was missing the point. He held up his backpack and tugged on the pocket with the open zipper. "What I wanna know is—who wrote it and who put it there?"

Red thought for a moment. "Do you remember who bought you that backpack?" he asked.

"Mom," said Ernie. It was an easy answer. Ernie's mom used to get all excited at the prospect of buying school supplies.

"So who do you think wrote the note?"

Ernie hesitated. "Mom?" he asked.

Red nodded slowly. "That's my guess," he said. "She loved you a lot. It makes sense to me."

Red put the note down and reached for the cupboard over the refrigerator where they kept the sugar and flour. He pulled down a large glass jar and eased open the lid. The jar was almost half full with yellow slips of paper. "Haven't you run across the notes she left around the house?" he asked. "Tucked in drawers and cupboards. I thought I'd found most of them but I guess that one was meant just for you."

"These are all notes from Mom?" said Ernie. He was amazed by the number of notes in the jar.

"She did this for years," his father laughed.

"How come I haven't run into them before?"

"Try cleaning your room," said Red, returning the jar to its shelf. "Try putting away your clothes. Try straightening up the—"

"Don't put away the jar just yet," said Ernie. "I want to read them."

Red stopped. Then he placed the jar on the counter and gave it a little push. "Knock yourself out," he said.

Ernie sat for a moment. He reached across the counter for the note in glitter and read the message to himself once. Then he folded the note and returned it to his backpack.

"'I know who likes you,'" said Red, already able to recite the note by heart.

"If you knew how much trouble that note got me into," Ernie began. "Everybody at school was freaking out—trying to figure out who wrote it."

"Like who did they suspect?" asked Red, with a significant look. "Like Swimming Pool?"

Ernie didn't say yes and he didn't say no. He threw Red a knowing look as though he wasn't going to answer either way.

Red chuckled. He picked up the box of macaroni and cheese. "Friendships change," said Red, rattling the noodles before he ripped open the box. "It's hard to stay friends when you're growing up and things are changing all the time. New friends come along. Old friends fade back but then they step up to bat again and become better friends than before. You can't predict what's going to happen with friends."

Ernie looked vaguely blank and confused.

"Did I solve that mystery?" Red asked with another chuckle. He switched the heat back on under the pot of water.

"I guess so," said Ernie.

"So you want some macaroni and cheese?"

"It's a pool party, Dad," Ernie protested, reaching for his backpack. "You want me to get cramps and drown?"

"No, no, no," said Red with a laugh. "I don't want that to happen."

Ernie headed for the door but turned back to lean against the counter.

"Hey, Dad," said Ernie, as though there was another question to follow.

"Shoot," said Red.

"When you're friends with Cat Lady," Ernie ventured, "do you call her 'Cat Lady'? Or 'Catherine'?"

Red snorted and barked with laughter. He caught Ernie by surprise. "I gotta tell you," he said. "It's happened! I called her Cat Lady to her face! I get that so confused!" Red started laughing harder still. In fact, he was laughing so hard that he turned red in the face and had to brace himself on the counter.

Ernie didn't think his question was that funny but he found himself laughing too. And they were still laughing when the water began to boil.

Swimming Pool tried to stay out of the way during the last-minute preparations for her eleventh birthday party. She sat in the chair in her bedroom with her ankles politely crossed while she waited for the company to arrive.

When Swimming Pool came downstairs to greet her guests, the only hullabaloo over her birthday was the above-ground pool, a birthday cake decorated to look like a pool, eleven candles—and that was about it.

"Perfect," said Swimming Pool. "It's just what I always wanted."

Dusty later admitted to Ernie that he'd been tempted to throw in lots of "tiki torches, ukuleles and—you know, that pig with an apple stuffed in its mouth?" Ernie tried to picture the birthday party with a dead pig and rolled his eyes. "But," Dusty resolved as he adjusted his snorkel, "Swimming Pool said simple, so simple it is." With that, Dusty took a deep breath and submerged.

Ernie was floating on a raft in the middle of Swimming Pool's pool. Betty had crawled onto Kip's shoulders to face off against Kirsten and Ronjon in a chicken fight. Gina was checking the chemical balance of the water. Noah Morgenstern was helping Finny and Fanny fit into their waterwings. And Swimming Pool herself was bouncing on the tip of the diving board, gauging the tension.

Red and Cat Lady stopped by to say hello—but they kept it short so that they wouldn't spoil the party.

"Brian should be able to keep an eye on you kids," said Red, whacking Swimming Pool's brother on the back of the head. Brian sat in a lounge chair on the deck with his nose buried in a comic book.

"Happy birthday, Swimming Pool," said Betty, creating just enough of a distraction in the chicken fight for Kirsten to knock her off Kip's shoulders and into the water. The laughter that followed was interrupted by a mild commotion from inside the house. The children looked in that direction, figuring it was time for cake. But instead what they witnessed was the arrival of Miss Ginger.

"Miss Ginger?" Kirsten gasped—just before Betty got her revenge by knocking Kirsten in the water.

"Miss Ginger?" said Gina, as though her presence at this party was highly improbable.

"Miss Ginger?" said Dusty, surfacing in his snorkel for a good look at the notorious charm queen.

"Yowza," said Betty, "I can't believe your mom invited Miss Ginger!"

"She didn't," said Swimming Pool. "I did."

"You?" said Betty, more than a little incredulous. "After everything Miss Ginger put you through?" Somehow this was incomprehensible.

"I'm eleven now," said Swimming Pool. "I'm too old to carry a grudge."

"But I thought you were afraid of Miss Ginger," said the girl with the braids and braces.

Swimming Pool shot her a look that said, "ix-nay!" as Miss Ginger took long, purposeful strides across the deck and called out, "Swimming Pool! Happy Birthday!"

"Miss Ginger!" cried Swimming Pool. "How kind of you to attend! Make yourself at home and I hope you brought your swimsuit!"

Miss Ginger was wearing a yellow pantsuit. She fussed her hands at Swimming Pool as though she wouldn't dream of getting wet. "Don't you be so silly," said Miss Ginger. "I just stopped by to help your mother light all those candles on your cake!"

With that, Miss Ginger followed Swimming Pool's mom inside.

"When did you and Miss Ginger get to be so friendly?" asked Ernie.

"We didn't," said Swimming Pool. "We're just practicing charm!"

Swimming Pool reached over the edge of the diving board to grab onto Dusty's snorkel so that he had to come up for air. She splashed water at Ernie to get his attention. "Come on up here," she said. "Both of you. I got a surprise."

Ernie and Dusty inched onto the diving board alongside Swimming Pool. It was a tight fit so they had to grab one another's hands for balance. "What's up, Swimming Pool?" said Ernie.

"If it wasn't for you guys, this birthday party wouldn't have been possible," Swimming Pool said.

"You get credit too," said Dusty.

"Friends again?" asked Swimming Pool.

"The best of friends," said Ernie.

"Excellent!" said Swimming Pool. "So why don't we celebrate this birthday with the biggest cannonball ever?"

Ernie and Dusty laughed. Together, they began to bounce on the diving board. "One-two-three—"

At that very same moment, the screen door opened and Miss Ginger came breezing onto the deck with her long, purposeful strides. Swimming Pool's mom followed with napkins, forks, and plates.

Miss Ginger marched right to the edge of the pool carrying Swimming Pool's birthday cake. Eleven candles, burning bright. "Swimming Pool," she cried, in her singsong way, "it's

Happy Birthday! Time to sing Happy Birthday!" But when Miss Ginger looked, Swimming Pool wasn't on the diving board. She wasn't on the deck. And she wasn't in the pool.

Miss Ginger happened to look up. And that's when she saw Swimming Pool, Ernie, and Dusty—the whole threesome—suspended in the air only a foot above the water and just about to make a gigantic birthday splash.

RULES OF FRED

It doesn't matter
Whose house you're in.
Use your fork
And wipe your chin.

Don't eat with your fingers.
That's against the law.
And just be grateful
You don't have a claw.

Napkins are handy
For the spill you just did.
But please do not mention
The lobster bib.

It's good at a party
To raise a toast.
And never forget
To thank the host.

Saying "please" really counts
In polite society.
Even oysters say "thank you"
And they live in the sea.

Respect your elders
And do as you're told.
You'll get to have payback
When you grow old.

If you use your best manners,
A good time will be had.
But if you act rude,
Face it. You're a crab.

DUSTY'S
PEANUT BUTTER COOKIE RECIPE

What you need:
Two big bowls, a wooden spoon, a measuring cup, an
ungreased cookie sheet, an oven, and an adult. Makes
maybe two dozen, depending on whether they burn.

1 cup peanut butter
  Regular works better than health food store variety.

½ cup butter
  Let it get soft. The cold brick is impossible.

½ cup white sugar

½ cup brown sugar

1 egg
  Get help if you can't crack it.

3 tablespoons milk

1 teaspoon vanilla extract

1¼ cups all-purpose flour

1¾ teaspoon baking powder
  Not baking soda. Trust me.

A pinch of salt

Directions:

1. Get your adult to preheat the oven to 375° F. Don't mess with the oven unless you've got an adult.

2. Mix the peanut butter, the butter, the white sugar, and the brown sugar until it's a good brown mash.

3. Add the egg, the milk, and the vanilla extract—one at a time. Keep mixing until it's all blended.

4. Combine the flour, baking powder, and that pinch of salt in another bowl. Add this mixture into the batter—but a little at a time, like papier mâché.

5. When the batter is mixed, roll a tablespoon of dough into a ball—and place it on the ungreased cookie sheet. Give each ball plenty of room. Press a fork into the ball to mash the cookie—but don't go crazy. Just a gentle smoosh.

6. Bake for 8–10 minutes in the oven—but check them from time to time because if the edges get slightly browned, your cookies are done!

7. Cool the cookies on a rack.

8. Clean up or get yelled at.